"YOU CAN'T STOP ME FROM TRYING TO ESCAPE!"

Dominic Lyall eyed her coldly. "I wouldn't advise it," he warned, leaning heavily on his cane.

A strained, tired look washed over his features. With a pang, Helen suddenly saw that standing so long fatigued him. So her captor was not as invulnerable as he would like her to believe!

A traitorous feeling of compassion stirred within her. She longed to know what had made him spurn the glamorous world he had known. Why had he buried himself away in the snowy wilds with only his torturing memories to haunt him?

HARLEQUIN CELEBRATES

Thirty-five Years of Excellence

1 **General Duty Nurse**
2 **Hospital Corridors**
3 **Court of the Veils**
4 **The Bay of the Nightingales**
5 **Leopard in the Snow**
6 **Dakota Dreamin'**

These books may be available at your local bookseller.

Don't miss any of our special offers. Write to us at the
following address for information on our newest releases.

Harlequin Reader Service
P.O. Box 52040, Phoenix, AZ   85072-2040
Canadian address: P.O. Box 2800, Postal Station A,
5170 Yonge St., Willowdale, Ont.   M2N 6J3

Anne Mather

Leopard in the Snow

Harlequin Books

TORONTO • NEW YORK • LONDON
AMSTERDAM • PARIS • SYDNEY • HAMBURG
STOCKHOLM • ATHENS • TOKYO • MILAN

Original hardcover edition published in 1974
by Mills & Boon Limited

ISBN 0-373-15105-5

Harlequin Presents edition published December 1974
Second printing May 1975
Third printing December 1977
Fourth printing March 1978
Fifth printing May 1978

Harlequin Celebrates Thirty-Five Years of Excellence
edition published November 1984

CHAPTER ONE

IN spring and high summer the lofty fells and mountain-shadowed lakes echoed with the sounds of tourists, eager to escape from the steel and concrete jungles of the cities. They came in their thousands, car after car, picnicking and camping, and towing their caravans behind them like an invasion of giant snails. Climbers, many of whom had never before put on spiked boots, trekked to Wast Water and Skafell Pike. Traffic jammed the narrow roads which skirted the more frequented lakes like Ullswater and Windermere. There were card shops and gift shops, and exhibitions of local crafts. On the lakes themselves the white sails of yachts mingled with orange-sailed dinghies and noisy outboard motors. Almost everywhere one looked there were people in parkas and sailing gear, all trying to look as though this was their natural habitat. The hotels were filled to capacity – the bars did a roaring trade.

And the locals watched and waited and longed for the city dwellers to return to their city homes and their city jobs, and leave the Lake District to those whose heritage it had always been.

It was that summer lakeland that Helen remembered. When they had had their home in Leeds her father had kept a boat at Bowness, and in the summer holidays when she was free from school, he had taught her to sail. In retrospect, it seemed an idyllic period in her life. It was in the days before her father became ambitious, before he allowed his small company to be amalgamated with Thorpe Engineering, before he married Isabel Thorpe and became such a rich and influential man with interests in more sophisticated sports than sailing . . .

But now the fells were clothed in snow. It had apparently been snowing for days, and even the lakes themselves had a film of white coating their surfaces. When she had stopped at the last village for directions to Bowness she had found herself well off her original route which wasn't altogether surprising when half the signposts had been covered with snow, too, and she had been too warm and snug in the car to bother to get out and wipe it away. She had been foolish, she acknowledged it now, but her memory did not go as far as recalling the dozens of minor roads that spun off the so-called major ones, and as they all looked much the same in these ghastly conditions she had obviously taken several wrong turnings.

Still, she consoled herself, with a glance at her wrist watch. It was only two o'clock and she had plenty of time to find a hotel before nightfall. Any hotel would do, just so long as it provided food and shelter. She could continue on her way tomorrow.

Tomorrow!

She spared a thought for her father. By tomorrow he would have discovered she had gone away. What would he do? Would her note that she needed to get away on her own for a while satisfy him, or would he institute some sort of search for her? The latter seemed the most likely. Her father was not the kind of man to be thwarted, and he would, no doubt, be furious that his daughter, his *only* offspring, should try to defy him.

But the chances of him discovering her here were slim. In fact, Helen congratulated herself, deciding to come north had been an inspiration. In recent years her most usual haunts had been the West Indies and the South of France, and if her father looked anywhere for her it would be somewhere warm. He knew how she loved the sun, how she enjoyed swimming and sailing, all water sports. He would never expect her to remember the small hotel where he had taken her as a schoolgirl in the years following her mother's death when they had been everything to one another. And he would certainly not expect her to drive into a raging blizzard . . .

The snow was thickening on her wiper blades, causing them to smear the windscreen rather than clear it. It seemed ages since she had passed another vehicle and she paused to wonder whether in fact the road she was following led anywhere. It might simply be the track to some farm or a private dwelling of some sort, and how on earth would she be able to turn in such a narrow space?

She frowned. If it was a farm track she would go and knock at the door and ask whether they could give her some firm directions as to how to reach the nearest village. She no longer expected to reach Bowness tonight.

The wipers got worse and with an impatient exclamation she stopped the car and leaving the engine running climbed out and brushed the snow away. It clung to her fingers. It was so cold, and with a shiver she clambered back inside again. Maybe she had been foolhardy in bringing the car. Perhaps she should have used the train. But she had not wanted to risk someone at the station recognising her and possibly remembering this when her father discovered she was missing and started making a fuss.

To her annoyance, the wipers stuck again, and she was forced to get out again and attend to them. She had taken off her long boots with their platform soles because they were impossible for driving and when she had attended to the wipers the first time she had balanced on the door valance. But this time she stopped to put her boots on and while she did so the engine idled to a halt.

Shaking her head, she got out and stood in the snow. It was quite deep, even on the road, and brushed the turn-ups of her flared scarlet pants. Drops of snow melted on her shoulders as she quickly cleared the snow from the windscreen and satisfying herself that the wipers would at least work for a short period, she got into the driving seat again.

It took several more minutes to divest herself of the boots again and then she turned the ignition. It revved, but nothing happened. Cursing silently to herself, she tried again, allowing it to go on for a long time, but still nothing happened. A pinprick of alarm feathered along her veins. What now? Surely the car wasn't going to let her down? It never had before. And it wasn't old. But it hadn't actually encountered conditions like these before.

Several minutes later she gave up the attempt to try and start the car again. It was getting later all the while and pretty soon it would start to get dark. She dared not risk staying here any longer in the vain hope that someone might come along and rescue her. There were no visible signs that anyone had passed that way that day although the steadily falling snow hampered any real inspection of the road's surface. Nevertheless, her most sensible course would be to leave the car and go in search of assistance, she decided. If she stayed where she was and no one came, the car could well be buried by morning and she had heard of motorists freezing to death in this way.

Thrusting such uncomfortable thoughts aside, she reached for her boots and began to pull them on again. It was quite an adventure, she told herself, in an attempt to lighten her spirits. Who would have thought when she left London this morning that by late afternoon she would be the victim of an abandoned car in a snowstorm? Who indeed? Her earlier self-congratulation that her father would never look for her here might rebound on her in the most unpleasant way possible.

She shook her head and got out of the car. At least her coat was warm. Made of red suede and lined with sheepskin, it showed up well against the whiteness of the snow. Maybe someone would see her, even if she didn't see them. She drew the hood up over her head, and tucked inside the long strands of black hair which the wind had taken and blown about her face. Well, this was it! Sheepskin mittens to warm her hands, her trouser legs rolled up almost to the knee, her handbag – what more could any intrepid explorer want?

She looked up and down the deserted road. There seemed no point in retracing her tracks. She knew there was nothing back there – at least, not for miles. Forward it would have to be!

The snow stung her cheeks, and the wind whistled eerily through the skeletal branches of the trees and bushes that hedged the track. She was tempted to penetrate the

9

hedge and climb the sloping fields beyond in an attempt to see some form of habitation in this white wasteland, but a preliminary reconnaissance landed her in snow at least two feet deep and was sufficient to deter any further forays in that direction. It wasn't possible, she told herself, that one could walk so far without encountering either a house or another human being, but she had. This winding road which had quickly hidden the car from view might be circling a mountain for all she knew. Certainly she was going uphill, her aching legs told her that, but what alternative had she?

She stopped and looked back. It was impossible to distinguish anything beyond a radius of a hundred yards. She was totally and completely lost and the greyness in the sky was not wholly due to the appalling conditions. Evening was approaching and she was no nearer finding a place to stay than she had been an hour ago. A fluttery sense of panic rose inside her. What was she going to do? Was this how fate repaid her for challenging her father's right to choose her a husband?

Something moved. Out of the corner of her eye she could see a movement, a trace of some colour up ahead of her. She blinked. What was it? An animal probably, foraging for food. Poor creatures. What could any animal find beneath this all-covering blanket?

Shielding her eyes, blinking again as snow settled on her lashes and melting ran down into her eyes, she tried to see what it was that had caught her attention. It was an animal, that much she could see, and no doubt her red coat had attracted its attention, too. It might be a dog, she thought hopefully, with an owner close at hand. Oh, please, she begged silently, let it be a domestic animal!

The creature was loping towards her. It looked like a dog. It was a curious tawny colour, and as it drew nearer she saw that it had splashes of black, too. A sort of tawny Dalmatian, only there weren't such things.

Then her legs went weak. She felt sick with fear. Panic crawled to the surface. It was no dog. It was no domestic animal. It was a *leopard*! A leopard in the snow!

For a moment she was rooted to the spot. She was mesmerised by that silent, menacing gait. She moved her head helplessly from side to side. There were no leopards in Cumberland! This must be some terrible hallucination brought on by the blinding light of the snow. The creature made no sound. It couldn't be real.

But as it got closer still, she could see its powerful shoulders, the muscles moving under the smooth coat, the strong teeth and pointed ears. She imagined she could even feel the heat of its breath.

With a terrified gasp she did the thing she had always been taught never to do in the face of a charging animal, she turned to run. In the days when she was a teenager, she had sometimes gone to stay with a friend from boarding school whose parents had kept a farm. They had taught her that to show any animal panic only inflamed the creature's senses, but right now she knew only a desperate desire for self-preservation.

She stumbled through the deep snow at the side of the road and forced her way through the hedge, feeling the twigs tearing at her hair, scratching her cheeks painfully. But anything was better than the thought of the leopard's claws on her throat and panic added its own strength to

11

her weakened limbs. The field was a wilderness of white, the deepness of the snow hindering her progress. Any moment she expected to feel the animal's hot breath on her neck, its paws weighing her down. Sobs rose in her throat, tears sprang to her eyes. She should never have left London, she thought bitterly. This was what came of behaving selfishly.

Beneath the snow her foot caught in a rabbit hole and she lost her balance and fell. Sobbing, she tried to crawl on, but as she did so she heard a sound which she had been beginning to think she would never hear again. That of a human voice – a human voice shouting with all the curtness of command: "*Sheba!* Sheba – heel!"

Helen's shoulders sagged, and she glanced fearfully over her shoulder. The leopard had halted several feet away and was standing regarding her with disturbing intensity. A man was thrusting his way through the hedge, a tall lean man dressed all in black – black leather coat, black trousers, and knee-length black boots. His head was bare and as Helen scrambled to her feet she saw that his hair was so light as to appear silver in some lights. Yet for all that his skin was quite dark, not at all the usual skin to go with such light hair. There was something vaguely familiar about his harshly carved features, the deep-set eyes beneath heavy lids, the strongly chiselled nose, the wide mouth with its thin lips that were presently curved almost contemptuously as he approached her. And she saw as he climbed the ridge that he walked with a distinct limp which twisted his hip slightly.

The leopard turned its head at his approach and he put down a hand and fondled the proud head. "Easy, Sheba!"

he murmured, his voice low and deep, and then he looked at Helen. "My apologies," he said, without sounding in the least apologetic, "but you ought not to have run. Sheba wouldn't have touched you."

His contempt caught Helen on the raw. She was not used to having to run for her life, nor to feeling distressed and dishevelled in the face of any man. On the contrary, her warmth and beauty, the silky curtain of dark hair, her slender yet rounded figure, had all made her contacts with men very easy relationships, and although she wasn't vain she was not unaware of her own attractiveness to the opposite sex. But the way this man was looking at her made her feel like a rather ridiculous child who had trespassed and found herself facing rather more than she had bargained for.

"How can you say that?" she demanded, annoyed to find that her voice had a tremor in it. "If you hadn't called as you did just now, I might have been mauled! "

He shook his head slowly. "Sheba is trained to bring down her prey, not to maul it! "

"I wasn't aware that I was prey! " retorted Helen, brushing the snow from her sleeves.

"You ran."

"Oh, I see." Helen tried to sound sarcastic. "I'll try to remember not to do that in future."

The man's hard face softened slightly with mocking amusement. "We didn't expect to find anything worth hunting today."

Helen drew an unsteady breath. "You didn't! "

"You underestimate yourself." He glanced round. "Are you making a walking tour of the fells?"

Helen's cheeks flamed. "My car has broken down back – back there." She gestured vaguely towards the road. "I – I was trying to find help, when – when your leopard –"

"Sheba?" The man glanced down at the big cat which stood so protectively beside him. "Sheba is a cheetah, not a leopard, although I suppose they're members of the same family. A cheetah is sometimes calling the hunting leopard."

"I really don't care what she is," said Helen tremulously. "Could – could you direct me to the nearest phone box and I'll try and make arrangements to be picked up?"

The man smoothed the cheetah's head. "I regret there are no phone boxes within walking distance."

"Then – then private houses – someone who has a phone!"

He shrugged. "There are few dwellings about here."

Helen clenched her fists. "Are you being deliberately obstructive, or is this your normal way of treating strangers?"

The man was annoyingly unperturbed by her rudeness. "I'm merely pointing out that you're in a particularly isolated area. However, you're welcome to my hospitality if such a thing is not abhorrent to you."

Helen hesitated. "I – I don't know who you are."

"Nor I you."

"No, but –" She chewed uneasily at her lower lip. "Are you married?"

His eyes narrowed. "No."

"You live – alone? Apart from this – this creature?"

"No." He moved as though standing too long in one

14

place made his leg ache. "I have a manservant. There are just the two of us."

Helen digested this. Oh, lord, she thought, what a situation! Faced with two impossible alternatives. Either to continue walking in these awful conditions in the hope that sooner or later she would come upon a shepherd's croft or a hill farm, which was a decidedly risky thing to do. Or to accompany this man – this stranger – to his home, and risk spending the night with *two* strange men. What a dilemma!

"Please make up your mind," the man said now, and Helen thought she could see lines of strain around his mouth. This outward sign of vulnerability decided her.

"I'll accept your hospitality, if I may," she murmured, with ill grace. "Ought I to go back for my suitcases?"

"Bolt will get them," replied her companion, beginning to descend the slope to the hedged road. "Come. It will be dark soon."

Helen licked her lips. "Ought – oughtn't we to introduce ourselves?"

The man gave her a wry look. "I think it can wait, don't you? Or are you enjoying getting soaked to the skin?"

Helen sighed. There was no answer to that. Instead, she followed him down the slippery slope, taking care to keep a distance from the sleek body and long tail of the cheetah. Once on to the track again, for that was all it was now with the drifts of snow at either side, the cheetah stalked disdainfully ahead and Helen was forced to walk at the man's side. For all he limped, he moved with a certain grace, a certain litheness, which made her wonder if he had once been an athlete. Was that why his face had seemed momentarily familiar? Or was it simply that he reminded her of someone else – someone she knew?

Just beyond the bend in the road a narrower track left the main one and it was on to this narrower way that they turned. A sign, half covered with snow, indicated that it was a private road and Helen felt a twinge of nervousness. This man could be almost anyone. He could be taking her anywhere. He might even have lied about there being no callboxes or farms in the near neighbourhood.

As though reading her thoughts, he said: "If you would rather turn back, you're at liberty to do so. I shan't send Sheba after you, if that's what you're afraid of."

Helen moved her shoulders in a deprecating gesture. "I – why should I want to turn back?"

"Indeed." The man glanced sideways at her and she noticed inconsequently that he had the longest lashes she had ever seen on a man. Dark and thick, they shaded eyes that were a peculiarly tawny colour, like the eyes of Sheba, his cheetah. And like Sheba's, they were unpredictable.

The track wound upward steadily. They passed through a barred gateway, crossed some fields through which a track had been cleared, and climbed a stone wall, half hidden beneath the snow. Eventually, a belt of stark trees rose up ahead, and beyond them, no doubt concealed in summer when the trees were fully in leaf, Helen saw the house they were making for. It was a rambling kind of building, its stone walls shrouded with snow. Smoke was issuing from its chimneys, and there were lights in some of the downstairs windows. A grassy forecourt was just visible beneath the prints of man and beast, and this gave on to a cobbled area in front of the house.

Helen's companion stamped his feet and advised her to do likewise to shake the snow from their boots. Then he thrust open the studded wooden door and indicated that she should precede him inside. Helen glance apprehensively at Sheba. The cheetah was watching her with an unblinking stare, but as it seemed perfectly willing to remain by its master's side, she walked rather gingerly ahead of them into the hall of the building.

Warmth engulfed her and it was only then that she realised exactly how cold she was. The desolation, her terrifying encounter with the cheetah, her subsequent confrontation with its master – all had served to provide her with other matters to concern herself, but now in the warmth of that panelled hall she began to shiver violently and her teeth started to chatter.

Their entrance brought a man through a door at the back of the hall. Even in her shivering, shaking state, Helen could not help but stare at the newcomer. As tall as the man who had brought her here, and twice as broad, he was built on the lines of a wrestler, with massive shoulders and a completely bald head. The look he gave Helen was cursory before his gaze travelled to the man with her.

"You're late, sir," he announced, pulling down his shirt sleeves which had been rolled above his elbows. "I was beginning to get worried about you."

The man with Helen began to unbutton his coat, his eyes flickering thoughtfully over the shivering girl in front of him. "As you can see, we have a visitor, Bolt," he remarked, in his low attractive voice. "The young lady's car

17

is out of action some distance down the lane. After you've prepared us some tea, perhaps you'd go and retrieve her suitcases."

Bolt's expression as he listened to his master was rather like Sheba's, Helen thought uncharitably. They both behaved as though the safety and well being of the man they served were the most important things in the world.

"Of course, sir." Bolt's mouth moved in the semblance of a smile. "I gather the young lady will be staying the night. I'll prepare a room for her, shall I?"

"Thank you, Bolt." The other man threw off his leather coat to reveal a black silk shirt and waistcoat beneath. The manservant took his coat, and then his employer turned to Helen. "You may give your coat to Bolt, too. I assure you he knows how to handle wet garments without causing them any ill effects."

Helen was shivering so much she couldn't undo the leather buttons, and to her astonishment the man limped forward and brushing her cold hands aside unfastened the coat himself. Then he lifted his hands and slid it off her shoulders and the man Bolt caught it as it fell.

Helen shivered all the more. She resented the way he had taken control without her permission. She didn't know this man with his harsh face and mocking tongue, and nor did she want to. Something about him disturbed her, frightened her even. She told herself it was his limp, the way his hip twisted when he moved, the arrogance of the man. And yet the fleeting touch when his fingers had deposed hers had caused a shaft of fire to shoot up her arm almost as though his touch had burned her, and she was at once fascinated and repelled.

Bolt moved to open a door to their right. Realising that both men were waiting for her to make the first move, she walked jerkily into the room beyond, hugging herself tightly in an effort to stop the enervating shivering. She found herself in an enormous living room lit by two standard lamps and by the glow from a roaring fire in the huge grate. Logs had been piled on to the blaze and the room was redolent with the scent of pine. The floor was partially covered with rugs and as well as several dining chairs and a bureau there was a dark brown, tapestry-covered three-piece suite which, although it had seen better days, looked superbly comfortable. Some shelves to one side of the fireplace were well filled with books and paperbacks and magazines, and a tray on which reposed a bottle of Scotch, a decanter of what looked like brandy, and two glasses were set conveniently beside the armchair at the farther side of the fire.

The door closed as Helen was pondering those *two* glasses, and she flinched as the cheetah brushed past her to stretch its length on the hearth. She glanced round apprehensively, half afraid she was alone with the beast, to find the man limping towards her. The servant Bolt had apparently gone about his business.

"Won't you sit down?" he asked, indicating the couch in front of the fire, and after a moment Helen moved to perch uneasily on the edge of an armchair.

The man gave her a wry look, and then took the armchair opposite, stretching his long legs out in front of him with evident relief. After a moment, he turned sideways and took the stopper out of the decanter. "Some brandy, I think," he remarked quietly, with an encompassing glance in her direction. "You seem in need of – sustenance."

He did not get up to give her the drink but stretched across the hearth and Helen had, perforce, to take it. Brandy was not her favourite spirit, but she was glad of its warmth to take away the chill inside her. She sipped it slowly, and gradually she stopped shaking.

Her companion did not have anything to drink, but lay back in his armchair, his eyes half closed, surveying her with penetrating intensity. Before she had finished the brandy, Bolt returned with a tray of tea. He ousted the cheetah from its comfortable position on the hearth and set an occasional table in its place, putting the tray within easy reach of his master. Then he straightened, and said: "I'll go for the suitcases now, sir. If the young lady will give me her keys."

"Oh! Oh, yes, of course." Helen gave him a rueful smile and rummaged in her handbag. She produced the leather ring which held all her keys and handed it over. "I'm very – grateful, Bolt. It's about a mile down the road – the car, I mean."

Bolt nodded. "I'll find it, miss."

"Thank you." Helen wriggled a little further on to her chair. The brandy had done its work and she was beginning to feel almost normal again. This time tomorrow she might have reached Bowness and this whole episode would be simply a memory, something amusing to tell her friends when she got back to London.

After the door had closed behind Bolt, the man opposite sat up and regarded the tray. As well as the teapot and its accoutrements there was a plate of sandwiches and a rather delicious looking fruit pie.

"Milk and sugar, or lemon?" he enquired, the tawny eyes annoyingly disconcerting. But with her newly restored self-confidence, Helen refused to be intimidated.

"Milk, but no sugar, thank you," she replied, and as he poured the tea she went on: "Don't you think it's time we exchanged names?"

The man finished pouring the tea, added milk, and handed the cup to her. "If it's important to you," he conceded dryly.

Helen gasped. "You mean you would ask a complete stranger to share your house without caring what that person's name was?"

"Perhaps I consider the kind of person one is rather more important than one's name," he suggested, continuing to look at her, his eyes unblinking. "For example, I don't need to know your name to know that you're a rather headstrong young woman who doesn't always take the advice that's offered to her."

Helen flushed. "How can you know that?" she exclaimed scornfully.

He shrugged. "It's unusual, is it not, to find a young woman like yourself driving alone in conditions like these and apparently, as you've admitted you have suitcases with you, prepared to stay somewhere." He frowned. "You may have arranged to meet someone, of course, and yet you seem unconcerned at being delayed overnight."

Helen sipped her tea. "Women have been known to make journeys alone, you know," she retorted.

"In conditions like these? It's not usual."

"I – I may be a working girl – a representative of some sort."

"Who's lost her way?"

"Yes."

"Possible. But not probable."

"Why not?"

"I don't think you are a working girl."

Helen uttered an impatient exclamation. "Why not?"

"The way you spoke to Bolt. As though you were used to having people run about after you."

Helen sighed. She had the feeling that in any argument with him she would come out the loser. And he was offering her his hospitality, after all. Perhaps she could be a little more gracious in accepting it. It wasn't like her to behave so cattily. But something about him brought out the worst in her.

"All right," she conceded at last. "So I'm not a working girl. As a matter of fact, you're right. My name is Helen James. I'm Philip James' daughter."

"Should that name mean something to me?" he enquired, somewhat sardonically. She noticed he did not take tea but helped himself to a sandwich after she had refused. "I'm afraid I'm rather – out of touch."

He smiled and for a moment he looked years younger. Helen's lips parted. His face! Something about his face was familiar. She *had* seen it before – she was sure of it. But where? And when? And in what connection?

Forcing herself to answer his question even while her brain turned over the enigma endlessly, she said: "My father is Sir Philip James. His company won an award for industry last year. Thorpe Engineering."

The man shook his head. "I'll take your word for it."

Helen felt impatient. "And you? You haven't told me your name?"

"Tell me first what you're doing here – miles from the kind of civilization I'm sure you're used to."

Helen bit her lip. "As a matter of fact I – needed to get away on my own for a while. I needed time to think and my father will never dream of looking for me here."

The man frowned. "You mean – you've run away?"

"Hardly that. I left my father a note. He doesn't have to worry about me."

"But he will."

"Perhaps." Helen moved uncomfortably. "In any event, none of this need concern you. I'm only grateful that you came along as you did. I could have been in real difficulties if you hadn't."

"You could. You could have died out there – in the snow." His voice was low-pitched and for a moment Helen felt a tingle of remembered apprehension. "It was very foolish of you to let no one know where you were going. Don't you realise that your car could have been buried for days before anyone found it – or you? Tell me, why was it so important that you should get away?"

Helen felt indignant. "I don't think that's any business of yours."

"Nonetheless, I am curious. Satisfy the curiosity of one who no longer inhabits the world you come from."

Helen stared at him. What a strange thing to say! Surely even the remoteness of this district in winter did not cut one off completely from the outside world. Unless one

23

chose it to be so . . . She shook her head.

"My father wants to run my life for me," she said slowly. "But I'm twenty-two — and possibly too independent, as you implied. We — disagreed over a small matter."

"I don't think it can have been such a small matter to bring you more than two hundred miles in the depths of winter, Miss James, but never mind. I respect your desire to keep your personal affairs private."

Helen's mouth turned down at the corners. It was hardly a concession. Leaning forward to replace her empty cup on the tray, she said: "And you? Don't you find it lonely living here, miles from anywhere, with only Bolt for company?"

The man's thick lashes veiled his eyes. "I'm a most uninteresting individual, Miss James. Can I offer you more tea?"

Helen declined, pressing her lips together impatiently. "Why are you avoiding answering me?" she demanded.

"Was I doing that?" His tone was mild, but his tawny eyes were watchful.

"You know you were." Helen sighed, a frown drawing her dark brows together. "I know your face from somewhere. I'm almost sure I've seen you before — either in the flesh or on film!"

"You're very flattering," he mocked. "Isn't that usually the male's prerogative?"

Helen was annoyed to find that he could embarrass her. It was a new experience for her. "You know what I mean. I *have* seen your face before, haven't I?"

The man seemed bored by her assumption. He rose abruptly to his feet, pausing a moment to rub his thigh as though it pained him. Then he walked with his uneven gait across to the long windows and drew heavy wine-coloured velvet curtains over the frosted panes. Helen saw, in those moments before the world outside was hidden from view, that it was already dark and the driving flakes of snow filled her with a disturbing sense of remoteness. She should have asked for help in starting her car again instead of accepting the man's hospitality, whoever he was, she thought uneasily. With his directions, surely she could have driven to some small hotel or guest house. But she soon dismissed these thoughts from her mind. She was being ridiculously fanciful in imagining that there was anything sinister in the assistance being offered to her, and besides, she ought to be grateful – he had virtually saved her life!

He turned back to her. "Bolt shouldn't be long with your cases, then he'll show you where you're to sleep, Miss James. I have an evening meal at about eight o'clock. I trust you'll join me."

Helen shifted in her seat, a feeling of irritation replacing apprehension. He was clearly determined not to answer her questions. Her sudden movements caused the cheetah to raise its head and stare at her. The eyes turned in her direction were curiously like its master's, and tales of witches and warlocks and their familiars flashed through her brain. Who was this man who lived in such splendid isolation – who walked with a limp – who kept a wild beast for company? She had an absurd notion that she must have succumbed to the cold and collapsed out there in the snow and this was some fantastic nightmare preluding death . . .

She started violently at the horrific twist of her thoughts and the cheetah allowed a low growl to escape from its powerful throat. The man came towards them then, murmuring reassuringly to the animal, his eyes on Helen's troubled countenance.

"Is something wrong, Miss James?" he enquired, his voice as soft as velvet with an underlying thread of steel.

Helen shook her head, looking almost desperately about the lamplit room. It was a most attractive room, she had to admit, and not at all the sort of surroundings to inspire unease. It had a masculine austerity, an absence of anything frivolous, but that was only to be expected. There were hunting trophies on the panelled walls, swords in their scabbards and antique guns, and several pieces of ornamental design which Helen recognised as being valuable. The room gave an impression of quiet quality and distinction, and although some of the appointments bore the marks of well-use, they did not detract from its air of comfortable elegance. Whoever he was, he was not a poor man, but why he should choose to live as he did was beyond her comprehension. Was he a painter, a sculptor, an artist of some sort? Who else desired such a solitary existence?

And then a framed photograph on the wall behind the bureau caught her eye. She couldn't distinguish every detail from where she was sitting, particularly in this shadowy light, but what she could see was enough to realise that it was the blown-up picture of a car smash, a violent pile-up of men and machinery that churned up the road and threw fragments of metal into the dust-choked air. It was not a coloured photograph, but its perception was such that the ugliness and savagery of the crash were brutally unmistakable.

Her shocked gaze shifted to the man who was now standing so stiffly beside the couch. The tawny eyes were hard and narrowed and she knew he had intercepted her revealing concentration on the photograph. She also knew why he was suddenly so aloof. He had guessed that her earlier suspicions regarding his identity were suspicions no longer. He had been one of the drivers involved in that ghastly crash. But it had been no ordinary pile-up. It had taken place about six years ago, on the Nurburgring in Germany . . .

"I know who you are," she said, slowly, wonderingly. She got to her feet. "You're – Dominic Lyall, the racing driver!"

The stiffness went out of his lean body and he leant against the back of the couch, supporting himself with his palms on the braided tapestry cushions. "I am Dominic Lyall, yes," he conceded wryly. "But I'm no longer a racing driver."

"But you were." Helen stared at him. "I remember my father talking about you. He admired you tremendously before – before –"

"Before the crash?" His tone was bitter. "I know."

"But he thought – I mean –" She broke off, her brows drawn together in perplexity. "It was generally assumed – well, you disappeared. My father said – lots of people said –" She moved her shoulders uncomfortably, leaving the words unsaid.

"It was thought that I was dead?" He was ironic. "Oh, yes, I'm quite aware of that rumour. My injuries were extensive, and it suited me to foster such a belief. There's nothing more pathetic than a fallen idol who still tries to hog the limelight."

"But it wasn't like that," Helen protested. "The crash was a terrible accident. No one was to blame. The publicity –"

"Did I say I blamed myself?" he interrupted her, his voice cool and cynical.

"No. No, but –" She caught her lower lip between her teeth. "My father was such a fan of yours. He still has some pictures of you in his study. And there were thousands of others like him. Do you think it was fair to allow them to assume that you were dead?"

Dominic Lyall straightened, one long brown hand massaging his hip. "Do you think I'm not entitled to any privacy simply because for a time I lived in the public eye, Miss James?"

Helen didn't know how to answer him. "I wouldn't presume to make judgements, Mr. Lyall. All I'm saying is that it seems a pity that a talent such as yours should be denied to other aspiring drivers."

His lips twisted. "So much and no more." He ran his fingers over the light hair at the nape of his neck. "You wouldn't begin to understand, Miss James."

Helen held up her head. "You underestimate me, Mr. Lyall."

His smile held a kind of self-mockery. "Perhaps I do, at that. However . . ." He drew a deep breath. "However, it's unfortunate that your memory serves you so well. I should have thought a child of sixteen would have been more interested in popular music and its idols."

"I've told you – my father went to racing events. Sometimes I went with him."

"Oh, yes, your father." His eyes narrowed broodingly. "A curious anomaly."

"What do you mean?" His words troubled her a little.

Dominic Lyall moved his powerful shoulders in a deprecative gesture. "I should have thought it would have been obvious, Miss James."

"What would have been obvious?"

He regarded her with that denegrating unblinking stare. "Why, your recognising me, Miss James. A most – unfortunate occurrence. I'm afraid it means that you will not be leaving here in the morning, after all."

CHAPTER TWO

FOR several minutes there was complete silence in the room. Helen couldn't believe she had heard him aright, but something in that lean, harsh countenance warned her that she had.

"You – you can't be serious!" she said at last.

"I'm afraid I am, Miss James."

"But – but why? *Why?*"

"Surely that's obvious, too. I have no intention of laying myself open to the kind of publicity that the discovery of me living here would create."

Helen refused to admit to the sense of panic that was churning inside her. "But – but I wouldn't tell anyone," she protested, saying the words she had heard so many times on the films and in television when the central character was confronted by some fugitive from the law. But Dominic Lyall was not a fugitive from the law – only from the world!

"I'm afraid I couldn't take that risk." He shook his head. "I think the temptation to tell your father that the man he thought dead was alive and well and living in the Lake District would be more than you could stand."

"It – it wouldn't!" Helen twisted her hands together. "In – in any case, you can't keep me here! I – it's illegal!"

His smile was not pleasant. "Really?"

"But – but it's insane! I mean, my father will be looking for me!"

"You told me yourself he would never dream of looking for you here."

"Not initially, no. But if all else fails –"

"By then you will no doubt be free to go back to him."

She trembled. "What do you mean?"

"Simply that I intend to make arrangements to leave the country. Until I do, you will remain."

Helen gasped. "But that could take months!"

"Weeks, anyway," he conceded dryly.

The door opened suddenly behind her and she started nervously. It was the manservant, Bolt, who stood on the threshold, his massive shoulders coated with snow.

"Ah, Bolt, you're back." Dominic Lyall greeted the man with a warmth he had not shown to Helen. "Did you find the car?"

Bolt grinned. "Yes, sir. The suitcases are in the hall. If you'll give me a moment to shed my coat, I'll show the young lady to her room."

Dominic Lyall nodded. "Do that, Bolt. And by the way, our house guest's name is Miss James, Miss Helen James. She'll be staying with us rather longer than we expected."

Helen had no idea what message flashed between the two men, but Bolt's only show of surprise was a faint drawing together of his brows. He tossed Helen's keys and said: "Yes, sir."

"I'll take those," went on his employer, catching the keys as Bolt tossed them to him. "I'll explain the situation later, right?"

"Yes, sir."

Bolt was infuriatingly complacent, and Helen, standing

watching the two men, felt absurdly near to tears. This couldn't be happening to her. It really *couldn't*. Dominic Lyall wasn't seriously intending to keep her here until he made arrangements to leave the country, was he?

"I don't want to see my room!" she burst out tremulously. "You can't keep me a prisoner here, you can't!"

Dominic Lyall's mouth had a slightly cruel twist. "And how do you propose to prevent me?" he enquired, in a soft, menacing tone.

"I – I'll run away –"

"Again?"

"I'll go to the nearest farm – or village. I – I'll phone for help!"

"There are no phones here, Miss James."

"I mean – in the village."

"Do you know the way to the village?" Dominic Lyall asked quietly.

"It shouldn't be too difficult to find." Helen's voice broke.

"In these conditions?"

A sob rose in her throat. "You're mad! Mad!" She caught her breath. "I don't want to stay here. I just want to go to Bowness. I promise I won't tell a soul I've seen you. Just let me go!"

"I'm afraid that's impossible, Miss James." Her tormentor turned to Bolt. "We must move the car tomorrow. Before the thaw sets in."

Bolt nodded. "I'll see to it in the morning."

Helen felt a devastating sense of hopelessness. There seemed no way out of this bizarre situation. Out of her own mouth she had condemned herself. If she had not

32

told him of her flight from her father – if she had not recognised him – if, if, if . . .

"You can't stop me from trying to escape," she declared tremulously.

"I shouldn't advise it," Dominic Lyall commented, flexing his back muscles.

There was a definite look of weariness about him now and Helen realised with a pang that it was standing so long that tired him. She ought to have felt glad that he was not as invulnerable as he would like her to believe, but she didn't. A traitorous sense of compassion was stirring within her, and she wondered what it was that had made him spurn the world he knew for this almost ascetic isolation.

Bolt, too, was aware of his master's discomfort, and with the familiarity of years of service said with anxious reproof: "It's almost time for your treatment, sir. If you'll go down, I'll be with you as soon as I've shown Miss James to her room."

Dominic Lyall's expression showed vague self-derision as he looked across at Helen. "You see how it is with me?" he demanded bitterly. "I'm like an old piece of machinery that needs constant oiling, aren't I, Bolt?"

Helen's lips parted. "You're not old!" she exclaimed, unable to prevent herself.

"At least as many years older than you were when first you heard my name," he stated grimly, as a spasm of pain crossed his lean face. "If – you will – excuse me . . ."

He left the room limping heavily, his hip twisting in a grotesque distortion of itself. Bolt watched him go, an expression of such love and devotion on his face that

33

Helen felt almost an interloper. The cheetah, too, moved silently after its master and then Bolt turned back to her.

"One moment, miss," he said, unbuttoning his fur-lined overcoat and taking it off. "If you'll come with me."

Helen wanted to protest. She ought to protest. She should say all over again that this was crazy, that they couldn't keep her here against her will, that she would find some way to get away whatever they told her. But she didn't. Instead, she watched Bolt pick up her suitcases and then followed his enormous frame up the wide oak stair-case, her feet sinking into the pile of its leaf-brown and gold carpet.

Like the hall, the staircase was panelled, and halfway up there was a circular window overlooking the back of the house. It was difficult to see anything through the swirling flakes that were still falling, but the brilliance of the snow did give an artificial illumination to the scene.

At the top of the stairs, a long landing led in either direction. A balustrade overlooked the well of the hall below, and Helen silently admired a crystal chandel-ier suspended there. Bolt led the way along the landing to the right of the stairs passing several doors before halting at the room which was to be hers. He opened the door, switched on the lights and allowed Helen to precede him inside.

There was a soft olive green carpet on the floor and this colour was echoed in the olive and cream bedspread and the long wild silk curtains drawn across the windows. The furniture, the bed, the triple-mirrored dressing table, the wide wardrobe, were made of a dark mahogany,

34

slightly larger than life but not out of place in this high-ceilinged apartment. A radiator ran beneath the window and the room was beautifully warm.

Bolt stood down her suitcases and indicated a door near the wardrobe at the far side of the room. "The bathroom, miss," he explained, looking round to assure himself that everything was in order. "I've put hot water bottles in the bed and they can be refilled later if you need them."

Helen bit her lip. "Thank you, Bolt," she said, amazed at her calm acceptance of the situation. Then, as he moved to the door: "By the way . . ."

"Yes, miss?" He surveyed her politely even while she sensed his impatience to go his master.

"Are you – do you intend to – lock me in?"

Bolt half-smiled, and swung the door closed behind him, and only then did she see the key on her side of the door.

Now that the manservant was gone, Helen moved to the windows, drawing aside the curtains to peer out. Her room appeared to be at the back of the house, but apart from a few snow-clad trees there was little to be seen. She allowed the curtains to swing closed and turned to survey her domain.

She thought a trifle hysterically that no hotel bedroom could be more luxurious and no proprietor more concerned for the comfort of his guest than Bolt. It was ludicrous! The more she thought about it, the more fantastic it seemed. She smoothed her moist palms down the seams at the sides of her trousers. How long was she expected to stay here? How long would it take Dominic Lyall to settle his affairs to his satisfaction and leave the country?

She paced restlessly about the floor, trying to quell the panic that was rising again inside her now that she was alone. Did he really mean what he had said? Or had it been a deliberate ruse to frighten her for his own amusement? She doubted the latter somehow, and yet he was a cultured, civilised man! How could he so cold-bloodedly decide to detain her here against her will until it suited him to let her go? What kind of life had he led these past few years to destroy the pangs of his conscience?

She looked at her watch. It was after six o'clock. Dominic Lyall had said that he had a meal at eight. But right now she doubted her ability to eat anything. And where was he? What sort of treatment did Bolt mete out?

She stopped before her mirror and surveyed her dishevelled appearance without pleasure. Her trouser legs were creased from when she had rolled them up, her hair was wind-blown, and her cheeks bore the scratches she had received when she had plunged headlong through the hedge. She raised a trembling hand to touch a strand of silky black hair. What was she going to do?

An inspection of the bathroom assured her that there was no other means of access than from the bedroom and turning the key in her bedroom door she decided to take a bath. The bath itself was huge, white porcelain and standing on black iron legs. There was plenty of hot water from a gurgling tank and it was amazing how relaxed the scented water made her feel. She had found several jars of bath-salts on a glass shelf above the wash basin, and she had sprinkled them liberally before climbing in.

Eventually, of course, she had to get out again and after letting the water run away she wrapped herself in an enormous white bath towel and went into the bedroom to get some clean underclothes from her case.

But the case was locked and she remembered with irritation that all her keys were on the ring that was presently in Dominic Lyall's possession.

She stood hesitantly in the middle of the floor, wondering what she should do. She was tempted to go out on to the landing and shout for Bolt, but the vulnerability of her position made her think again. With ill grace she put on the clothes she had taken off and had to satisfy herself by doing her hair and applying a light make-up to her face. Her comb and cosmetics were, thankfully, in her handbag, and at least she did not look so dishevelled when she was finished. The white sweater she had worn with her slacks was reasonably smart and she doubted whether Dominic Lyall would notice anyway. All the same, she determined to have her keys before going to bed. She had no intention of sleeping without a nightgown.

A ripple of awareness ran through her at this thought. But there was no fear that anyone might disturb her in the night, she thought impatiently. Her door locked securely, and was heavy enough to thwart the most determined intruder. Besides, Bolt did not strike her as the sort of man to force his attentions on anyone, and Dominic Lyall . . .

She licked suddenly dry lips. She didn't want to think about Dominic Lyall, but it was impossible not to do so. She didn't want to remember the disruption of her senses when he had touched her earlier, or the fearful fascination he had inspired in her. It was repulsion, she told herself fiercely. She loathed and despised him. She couldn't

37

be attracted to a man like him, a *cripple*; a man moreover who had no compunction about twisting her plans to suit his own ends.

And yet she remembered every small detail about him — the curious lightness of his hair, the tawny eyes, and his dark skin, the lean strength of his body, the way the muscles of his thighs had been visible through the taut material of his black trousers, the knee-length boots, and the revealing anguish when he had been in pain. She caught her breath. She couldn't feel pity for him, she couldn't! But she did.

Shaking her head so that the heavy swathe of black hair swung confidingly beneath her chin, she unlocked the bedroom door and pulled it open. The landing stretched away before her, dimly lit and deserted. With a muffled exclamation, she switched off her bedroom lights and walked determinedly towards the balustrade at the head of the stairs.

In the hall below, she looked about her distractedly. Which door led into the living room? She couldn't remember. She approached what she thought was the living room and opened the door only to discover a downstairs cloakroom. She quickly closed it again and tried another, feeling a little like Alice must have felt down the rabbit hole. This room proved to be a small dining apartment with a blank cloth covering a circular table. Was this where she was expected to have her evening meal?

She sighed and then, hearing a sound behind her, spun round. A door across the hall had opened and Dominic Lyall was standing in the aperture, the cheetah, Sheba, at his heels.

"Won't you join me?" he invited, in the deep attractive voice she had come to know so well in such a short space of time, and with a helpless shrug she obeyed him.

He stood aside to allow her to enter the living room and then closed the door behind them. He had changed from his black clothes into a rich purple silk shirt, cream suede pants that moulded his lean hips, and a darker beige suede waistcoat. His face showed none of the strain which had been evident earlier, and Helen reflected that Bolt must have done his work well. He had the build of a wrestler, but he could be a masseur.

She moved across to the fireplace, keeping an alert eye on the cheetah following her. The fire had been built up with logs in her absence and the occasional table where they had had their tea was now spread with a cloth.

Dominic indicated the armchair she had occupied before. "Please – sit down," he said. "Can I offer you a drink before supper?"

He might have been addressing an expected guest, and Helen felt a rising frustration. Did he expect her to behave as though that was the case? Was she to offer no obstruction to his plans? How dared he assume that she had nothing to say in the matter?

"As a matter of fact I didn't come down to have supper with you!" she declared, saying the first thing that came into her head. "I want my keys – the keys to my suitcases. You have no right to keep them. I couldn't even get a change of clothes after taking a bath!"

Dominic frowned, thrusting a hand into his trousers' pocket and bringing out the leather key-ring. He examined the assortment of keys thoughtfully, and then said: "I'm sorry. Naturally you want the keys to your suitcases. If you'll point them out to me . . ."

Helen stared at him mutinously for a few moments and then without stopping to consider the consequences she rushed forward and tried to snatch the keys from his hand. She didn't really know what she intended doing with them even if she had been successful. Wild ideas about running out into the night, starting her unstartable car and driving away, were pure fantasy. But she had to do something, anything, to show him that she was not as helpless as he imagined her to be.

Her efforts were doomed to failure. His fingers closed over the key-ring as she sprang forward, and all her frenzied attempts to prise them apart were useless. If she had supposed him weakened in some way, if she had thought that because of his disablement he no longer possessed the strength to withstand attack, she soon realised how wrong she had been. When she flew at him she had half expected him to lose his balance, but he didn't, and there was an unyielding resistance in his hard body. She was totally unaware that the cheetah was watching them with alert, intelligent eyes, prevented from intervening by a quiet command from its master, but as she continued to pry desperately at his fingers she could not help but be aware of Dominic Lyall. She could feel the heat of his body, she could smell the faintly musky scent that emanated from him, but when she looked up and saw the cruel smile of derision that was twisting his lips, she drew back with a dismayed gasp.

"You – you brute!" she cried tremulously. "They – they're my keys. I want them."

"Don't you think you're behaving rather foolishly?" he asked, raising eyebrows several shades darker than his hair. "I had already offered to give you the keys you wanted."

Helen moved her head from side to side in a hopeless gesture. "Why are you doing this?" she demanded, in a defeated voice. "Why can't you let me go?"

"Tonight?" he mocked.

"No. In the morning." She made one last appeal to him. "*Please!*"

"Don't plead with me," he exclaimed, contempt colouring his tone. "I despise weakness!"

Helen felt as though he had struck her. With a hand pressed to her throat she turned away from him, gripping the back of the couch in a desperate effort to gain control. Tears burned at the back of her eyes and she badly wanted to give in to them. She felt utterly lost and alone, incapable of any coherent thought. Not even the malevolent stare that Sheba was directing at her for daring to challenge her beloved master could arouse a spark of antagonism inside her.

"Here! Drink this!"

Dominic Lyall thrust a glass into her hand and she looked down at it blankly. "What is it?"

"Brandy," he replied briefly. "It may help to restore your common sense."

Helen was tempted to throw the glass to the floor and scatter its contents likewise, but she was badly in need of a restorative. Raising the glass to her trembling lips, she swallowed a mouthful jerkily and then finished it all in a sudden gulp. The spirit stung her throat and she coughed as tears came to her eyes, but she could feel its warmth tingling to the surface.

Dominic Lyall limped round the couch and without waiting for her to join him, seated himself in the armchair at the far side of the blazing fire. He poured himself some Scotch from the bottle on the tray beside his chair and then extracted a narrow cigar from a box on the bookcase nearby. He held a taper to the flames and lit his cigar with evident enjoyment, and Helen stood watching him from behind the couch wondering how he could behave so casually when he must know how she was feeling.

When his cigar was lit to his satisfaction, he put it between his teeth and felt in his pocket for her keys again. He examined them carefully, extracted two keys, and then tossed the others towards her. She was not quick enough to catch them and they fell on the floor at her feet. With a feeling of humiliation she bent to pick them up and saw that he had taken the car ignition key and the smaller key which opened the boot.

"Now," he said, stretching his long legs out in front of him, "are you going to sit down?"

Helen pressed her lips together. "No," she said unsteadily, "I'm going to my room. I shall just hope that by the morning you'll have come to your senses."

His smile held the mockery she had come to expect. "Don't be too disappointed if I haven't," he commented, removing the cigar from his mouth.

"I – I think you're despicable!"

"Your opinion of me isn't important." He watched her as she walked to the door. "And haven't you ever heard that a war is fought on the stomachs of its troops?
42

If you don't have any supper, you're going to be awfully hungry by the morning."

Helen stiffened her shoulders. At least in this she could decide for herself. "I – I couldn't touch your food!" she stated, anger strengthening her determination. "It would make me *sick*."

Before she could make a dignified exit on those words of finality, the door opened and Bolt entered the room carrying a tray. She couldn't see everything he was carrying, but the aroma of curry sauce was unmistakable and she observed a jug of cream that was intended to accompany a mouthwatering fruit pie that balanced on her side of the tray. The manservant looked at Helen in surprise, and then said:

"I thought I'd serve supper in here, sir, seeing that it's such a wintry night."

"A good idea," said Dominic Lyall, smiling with rather more amusement than usual. "Will you join me, Bolt?"

Bolt glanced at Helen again. She was still hovering by the door, almost hypnotised by the smell of food. She was only beginning to realise how ravenously hungry she was, and she half regretted her impulsive rejection of his hospitality.

"But I thought – the young lady –" he began, but Dominic shook his head.

"Msis James – isn't hungry, Bolt. She said something about feeling – sick?"

His eyes moved to Helen's uncertain face and their hardness moved her to action.

"That's right," she declared, her lower lip quivering in spite of her determination that it should not. "I – I'm

43

rather more particular who I eat with!" And she stalked out of the room, banging the door behind her.

She stood for a moment in the hall after the door had closed, half expecting him to come after her and take some retaliatory action. But all she heard was a burst of laughter which unmistakably issued from Dominic Lyall's throat, and she realised that the second glass on the tray was used by Bolt . . .

CHAPTER THREE

HELEN's bed was superbly comfortable, the hot water bottles reminding her of when she was a child and her mother used to tuck her up with a bedtime story. Only now there was no bedtime story, only the similarities between her plight and that of Beauty and the Beast . . .

She had not expected to sleep, but exhaustion had played its part and when next she opened her eyes the room was filled with the brilliance of sun and snow. For a few moments it was difficult to remember where she was, but all too soon the memories came crowding back to her. Not that she knew where she was exactly, unless a house in the Lake District constituted knowing one's whereabouts, but she did remember her host and the unreal events of the night before.

She brought her arm out of the bedclothes and looked at her watch. It was almost nine-thirty, and she blinked in surprise. Nine-thirty! She had slept over twelve hours!

Thrusting back the covers, she sprang out of bed and went across to the windows. Now that it was daylight she would be able to see where she was, possibly even glimpse some other habitation.

But her view was, from her point of view, depressingly disappointing. All she could see was the snow-covered garden at the back of the house and beyond fields of unbroken white. Directly below her windows, a yard had been cleared, no doubt by Bolt, and there were melting footprints suggesting that someone had already gone out.

She drew back the curtains and looked round the room. In daylight it was no less attractive, although the tumbled mess of clothing overflowing from her suitcases did look rather untidy. But last night she had been too upset to do anything but find a nightdress and tumble into bed.

Now she ignored the mess and went into the bathroom. She would have liked a shower, but there was no shower fitting and a bath would take too long. So she contented herself with a thorough wash, and then went back into the bedroom to find something to wear.

She was in the process of fastening orange corduroy jeans about her slender waist when there was a tentative knock at the bedroom door. Immediately her heart began to pound and she stood silently for a moment wondering who it could be.

"Miss James? Miss James, are you awake?"

Bolt's voice was reassuringly normal.

"Y – yes, I'm awake," she answered. "What do you want?"

"I've brought you some breakfast, miss. I thought you might be feeling hungry."

Helen hesitated. She was tempted to order him away, to tell him to give his master the message that she was on a hunger strike until they let her go. But somehow she sensed that such tactics would not work with a man like Dominic Lyall. He was quite likely to allow her to faint from exhaustion before he would trouble to show any concern. And even then she doubted whether he would give in.

"I – just a minute," she called, and reaching for an

emerald green sweater quickly pulled it over her head, releasing her hair from the rounded neckline as she opened the door.

Bolt stood outside, tall and broad and almost familiar. In his tartan shirt, the sleeves of which were rolled above his elbows to reveal the bulging muscles of his forearms, and loose flannels, anyone less like a housemaid could not be imagined, and yet the tray he brought into the room and set down on her bedside table was as neatly set as any woman could do it.

"Cornflakes, eggs and bacon, toast and marmalade and coffee," he announced, with a wry smile. "Is that all right?"

Helen looked down at the loaded tray and then up at Bolt, and a faint colour stained her cheeks. "It – it sounds marvellous!" she admitted honestly. "I'm starving!"

"Mr. Lyall thought perhaps you might be," remarked Bolt dryly, and Helen's lips tightened.

"Oh, he did, did he?"

Bolt sighed. "Now you're not going to tell me to take it all away again, are you?" he exclaimed.

Helen hesitated. "I'd like to," she muttered mutinously.

"Why cut off your nose to spite your face? It's no skin off Mr. Lyall's back if you choose to starve yourself."

Helen hunched her shoulders. "I know that."

"There you are, then. Don't be churlish. Eat your breakfast. I'll come back later for the tray."

Helen looked up at the husky manservant doubtfully. "How long does – he –" She refused to say *Mr.* Lyall.

"How long does he expect to keep me here?"

Bolt walked towards the door. "Eat your breakfast, miss," he advised quietly, and left her.

When the door had closed behind him Helen stared impotently at the panels. Why had she supposed that Bolt might feel a sense of compassion for her? She should have known it was useless to try and alienate his loyalties.

For the moment, however, the scent of fried bacon was too much for her. She lifted the perspex covers and was soon eating ravenously. Normally, toast and coffee was sufficient for her, but this morning she ate everything Bolt had provided, finishing with three sticky slices of toast and marmalade. The coffee was good, continental, she guessed, and when she had finished she felt marvellously replete.

Wiping her fingers and her mouth on her napkin, she rose from the side of the bed and walked once more to the window. What was she supposed to do now? Bolt had said that he would come back for the tray. Did that mean that she was expected to stay here, in her room?

Her whole being revolted against such an idea. In spite of the unpleasant aspects of her situation, it was a beautiful morning and she longed to be out in the clean air. She thought of the little hotel in Bowness she had been making for. She had planned to spend her days walking and motoring, enjoying the unaccustomed freedom from her father's increasingly possessive demands, but now it seemed she was in an even more difficult position, confined more convincingly than her father could ever have imagined.

Thinking of her father made her wonder if he had received her note yet. She had posted it in London the day before on her way north. She had not wanted any significant postmarks pointing the direction of her flight. Now she wished she had not covered her tracks so completely. Nobody would dream of looking for her here, and even if they did, how would they find her? If Dominic Lyall had lived here in solitude for the past few years, no one was likely to disturb that solitude now. In fact, she doubted that anyone was aware of his existence . . .

She frowned. But someone must be, she thought eagerly. Someone had to supply milk and eggs, and what about mail? Her spirits rose a little. If they intended keeping her here, feeding her, they would need more provisions, and perhaps whoever supplied their groceries would notice an increase in the order.

Then she heaved a sigh. Bolt could well tell storekeepers that they had a guest, and who was to dispute it? Her only chance in that direction seemed to be if someone should happen to come to the house. The postman, for example.

Refusing to be downhearted, she considered ways in which she might attract attention to herself. She was intelligent enough to realise that Dominic Lyall would not allow her to be seen, so therefore she had to contact assistance some other way. A note, perhaps, tossed from an upstairs window. No! It would either disappear beneath the snow or be completely invisible or the wind would gust it away. Perhaps that was an even better idea. Putting her name and the address . . . A sense of despair filled her. How could she put an address? She had no idea where she was – where this house was! It was useless. She couldn't even remember the name of the village where she had asked for directions the previous day.

Another wave of hope washed over her. The people at that village. The Postmaster! He might remember a strange young woman asking for directions. Surely there were not so many strangers about at this time of the year. Yes, if he was asked she was almost sure that he would remember. And he would be able to say which way he had directed her.

Her hands clenched in her pockets. What lengths the mind would go to find a grain of hope in a hopeless situation. Who was she fooling? Everything hinged on her father looking for her, and he might decide to wait and see how long it would be before she returned. But if he did look for her, if he exhausted the places he might imagine she would go, if he suddenly thought of their holidays in the Lake District, if he came north and found the village where she had asked directions . . .

So many ifs. It was impossible. And as the days – maybe even weeks – went by, the postmaster at that tiny village store would surely forget. And even if he remembered, she had taken so many turnings after leaving there that she could be in any number of places.

There finally remained publicity. Her father might get sufficiently worried about her to give the story to the press. If her picture was on the front page of every paper in the country, maybe someone might remember her . . .

A knock at her door again disturbed her.

"Yes?" she called.

Bolt opened the door and put his head round. "Have

you finished?"

Helen nodded, indicating the empty tray. "Yes, thank you. It was delicious. I'm afraid I've been very greedy."

Bolt grinned. "Good. Everything looks brighter on a full stomach."

"You think so?" Helen was dry.

"Undoubtedly." Bolt opened the door wider and came into the room. "Are you coming downstairs?"

"Am I allowed to do so?"

"You can please yourself, miss."

"Can I?" She moved her shoulders irritatedly. "Where – where is your employer?"

Bolt picked up the tray. "In his study, miss. I shouldn't disturb him."

Helen raised her eyes heavenward. "Did you think I might?"

Bolt shrugged. Then he looked at her untidy suitcases. "I'll attend to your things later, when I make the bed."

Helen was horrified. "No – I mean, don't bother."

"It's no bother, miss."

"I can do them."

Bolt made no reply to this. Instead, he walked to the door. "It's a beautiful morning. Wouldn't you like to go outside?"

Helen stared at him. "Outside?" She shook her head helplessly. "What would – that man say to that? I might escape."

Bolt's expression was sardonic. "I wouldn't advise you to try, miss. Sheba's trained for hunting deer. I shouldn't like to see you as her prey."

Helen made an involuntary exclamation. "Then it's as

well you weren't with us yesterday," she retorted, shivering at the remembrance of that nerve-tingling experience.

"Yes, miss, so I heard," remarked Bolt, and with a slight nod of his head he left her.

Helen took one look round her room and then followed him, down the broad panelled staircase and into the sunlit hall below. Bolt went through a baize-covered door at the back of the stairs, and on impulse she followed him.

She found herself in an enormous kitchen. The tiled floor was scrubbed and shining, and although it had been extensively modernised with steel draining boards and a steel sink, there remained the huge range which had once provided the only cooking facilities, and a black-leaded fireplace where logs sparked cheerfully. An open door gave a glimpse of a cold store, but there were no hams hanging from the ceiling, only a coffin-like deep-freezing cabinet. All the same, the kitchen was a homely room and Helen looked about her with genuine interest.

Bolt deposited her tray on the draining board and began unloading the dirty dishes into the sink. He gave Helen a brief grin and said: "I expect you think this is a strange job for a man, don't you?"

Helen lifted her shoulders indifferently, moving towards the scrubbed wooden table that occupied the centre of the floor. Tracing the grain with her fingernail, she said honestly: "I don't think it's such an odd occupation for a man nowadays, but I must admit, you don't look the part."

Bolt chuckled. "No, I don't suppose I do."

Helen looked up. "But it hasn't always – well, I mean, this isn't your only occupation, is it?"

"It is now." Bolt plunged his hands into the soapy liquid in the sink. "But I guess you could call me a Jack-of-all-trades. I was in the Army to begin with – joined when I was just a kid. Then when I left the service I was a wrestler for a time. But I got bored. Nothing to it, you see. So I became a motor mechanic." He paused. "Now I'm a housekeeper."

"You're very – fond of your employer, aren't you?" Helen ventured.

"He's a fine man," he replied with quiet determination.

"Yes." Helen digested this. "Well, you'll pardon me if I reserve judgement." She frowned. "Have – have you known him long?"

"Twenty years, give or take a month or two."

"But you haven't worked for him all that time?"

"For him – with him – who cares? His father was my commanding officer when I was in the Army."

"I see."

Helen moved to the draining board. Wide windows overlooked the yard at the back of the house, flanked about with sheds and outbuildings.

"Tell me," she said, with what she hoped was only casual enquiry in her voice, "how do you get supplies? Fresh things like milk and eggs – and the mail?"

"Well, the mail is collected from a poste restante address," replied Bolt calmly, quietly dashing any hopes she might have had in that direction. "And we have a couple of cows and some chickens, and in the summer we grow our own fruit and vegetables and deep-freeze them for use later on. We're pretty self-sufficient. I even make my own bread. Why?"

"Miss James is speculating on ways of outwitting us, Bolt," remarked a lazily sardonic voice behind them, and Helen swung round to find Dominic Lyall resting negligently against the door jamb. He had returned to his black attire and in spite of the silvery lightness of his hair he had a disturbingly satanic appearance. He inclined his head politely towards Helen, and went on: "Good morning, Miss James. I trust you slept well. Bolt tells me you were ready for your breakfast. Did you enjoy it?"

Helen would have loved to have been able to say that she hadn't touched his food, but that, of course, was impossible. Instead, she took a defiant stance. "Just what do you think my father will do when he eventually discovers that you kept me here against my will?"

Dominic straightened. "I imagine it could create difficulties for you."

"For me!" Helen was aghast. "For you, you mean!"

"Why should it create difficulties for me? I won't be around. You will."

"Do – do you think he'll let it rest there?" Helen warmed to her subject. "He'll find you, wherever you are!"

"Oh, really?" Dominic's eyes were mocking. "Forgive me if I doubt your father's investigative powers. If the whole of the press media were unable to discover my whereabouts several years ago, I somehow can't drum up a great deal of anxiety about your father's efforts."

"He – he can give the story to the press! He can afford any number of detectives."

"Can he?" Dominic stroked his sideburns thoughtfully. "That's interesting. And this from someone who only yesterday was endeavouring to assure me that should I allow her to leave she would mention my whereabouts to nobody."

Helen's cheeks burned. "I meant what I said."

"Did you? But now you've changed your mind."

"Yes. No. I mean –" She sought for words. "I'm only trying to show you that if you thwart my father you'll have to pay for it."

"Threats, Miss James?"

Helen shook her head impotently. "Stop tying me up with words. If you let me go, I'll forget you're here. If you don't – well, I can't be held responsible for the consequences."

Dominic's lips twitched. "Yes. Very interesting, I'm sure." He looked across at Bolt. "Do you think we could have some coffee? I'm taking a break for a few minutes."

"Of course," Bolt nodded, and Helen scuffed her feet, feeling ridiculously petulant and childlike.

Dominic regarded her sulky face tolerantly. "Will you have coffee with me?" he suggested mildly, and she glared at him.

"I'm not thirsty!" she stated rudely.

"As you like."

Dominic shrugged and went out, letting the door swing closed behind him. Contrarily, as soon as he had gone, Helen wished she had not been so hasty. Her only chance of escape lay in persuading him to change his mind and so long as she was behaving like a spoilt schoolgirl what possible opportunity had she for doing that?

She perched moodily on the edge of one of the wooden

55

chairs which faced the scrubbed table and watched Bolt plugging in the coffee percolator, setting a cup and cream and sugar on a silver tray. His gaze flickered over her once and then, as though taking pity on her, he said: "Do you want to take it through?"

She looked up. "What do you mean?"

"You know what I mean. The tray. The coffee. Do you want to take it to Mr. Lyall?"

Helen hunched her shoulders. "If you like," she agreed offhandedly.

Bolt considered her flushed face. "Do you want a bit of advice, for what it's worth?"

She frowned. "What kind of advice?"

"Just go easy on the threats, will you? Mr Lyall isn't the kind of man to take that sort of attitude lightly."

"Oh, really?" Helen resented his assumption that Dominic Lyall must always be obeyed. "And what do you expect me to do? Sit back and wait until he decides to let me go?"

"It might be the best thing to do."

"You've got to be joking!"

Bolt shrugged his massive shoulders. "Don't underestimate him, Miss James. Don't make the mistake of thinking that because of his – disability, Mr. Lyall is any less of a man!"

Helen's cheeks burned as she got to her feet. "I don't see your point."

"I think you do, you know." Bolt unplugged the bubbling percolator and filled the coffee pot which was set on its own small burner to keep its contents steaming hot. "Just because he chooses to live here without a woman

56

it doesn't mean that he lacks the normal needs of any virile male!"

Helen's fists clenched. "I should have thought that you could satisfy all his needs, Bolt!" she declared offensively, but Bolt merely gave her a long and steady appraisal.

"No, Miss James," he replied quietly. "Mr. Lyall is not that kind of a man."

Helen didn't know where to look. She had never behaved so badly before, and the knowledge that Bolt, who had shown her nothing but kindness, should bear the brunt of her ill-conceived outburst filled her with shame.

"Oh – I'm sorry!" she exclaimed, pressing her palms to her hot cheeks. "That was – unforgivable."

Bolt put the lid on the coffee pot and pushed the tray across the table towards her. "You're overwrought," he explained gently. "Calm down. Nothing's ever as bad as we anticipate. Now – are you going to take the coffee through to Mr. Lyall. You'll find him in the living room. I've put out two cups just in case."

Helen's hands fell to her sides and her mouth tilted slightly at the corners. "You never give up, do you?"

"Let's say I'm basically optimistic," he commented, flexing his shoulder muscles. "Do you know which door you need?"

Helen nodded. "I think so." She picked up the tray and walked to the kitchen door. Then she turned. "And – thank you, Bolt."

He shook his head. "All part of the service, miss."

When Helen opened the living room door it was to find Dominic Lyall lying on the couch, his eyes closed. They flickered open at her entrance, however, and when he saw who was bringing in the tray of coffee, he swung his legs to the floor and tried to stand up. But a spasm of pain crossed his face as he did so, and he fell back against the cushions, a hand pressed in agony against his forehead.

Helen caught her breath and hurrying forward she set down the tray and said: "Are – are you all right?" in a concerned tone.

His hand fell to his side and his jaw was taut and bitterly self-derisive as he looked up at her. "Oh, yes," he muttered grimly, "I'm quite all right. Thank you."

Helen stood uncertainly staring at him, twisting her hands together anxiously. He looked so pale and strained that she longed to be able to do something for him. Seeing him like this in no way alleviated her own frustration at her enforced confinement here, although she realised that perhaps it should have done. They were enemies, after all, and she ought to feel some pleasure in knowing that fate could strike at him in other ways, but she didn't. All she did feel was a disturbing sense of compassion, and a growing awareness of his undoubted sexual attraction for her.

"For God's sake!" he bit out harshly. "Stop staring at me as if you'd never seen such a monstrosity before! I suffer from migraine, do you understand?" His lips twisted. "Among other things!"

Helen moved uncomfortably under that tawny gaze although she could see a faint glazing of the pupils of his eyes, and there were beads of sweat standing on his forehead after the exertion of trying to get up.

"I – is there anything I can do?" she suggested tentatively, and he gave her a scornful look.

"What do you suggest?" he demanded. "A gun at my temple, or a knife in my stomach?"

"Neither of those alternatives," she answered swiftly, looking helplessly round the room. "Don't you have anything to take? Some tablets, perhaps? Or shall I fetch Bolt?"

"I have tablets," he conceded at last, closing his eyes.

"Well, where are they?"

"You don't have to help me. Bolt can get them."

"For heaven's sake!" she exclaimed. "I'll get them. I want to. Just tell me where they are."

He half opened his eyes, resting his head back against the tapestry cushions. For a moment he looked at her through the thick veil of his lashes and it was a disturbing experience. She felt a devastating weakness attacking her lower limbs and a quickening of the blood through her veins. Then he closed his eyes again and said: "They're in a bottle in the top drawer of my desk."

Helen started forward and then halted uncertainly. His desk? Where was his desk? Did he mean the bureau in the corner, the bureau above which she had seen the revealing photograph of the accident? As she began to cross the room, he said wearily: "My desk is in my study."

His study!

Helen hesitated. Where was his study? She opened her mouth to ask him and then closed it again. It had to open off the hall and there were surely not so many doors left that she couldn't identify. If she remembered which was the cloakroom and which the dining room, and the kitchen door was covered with green baize.

She went quickly out of the room, thankful that the

59

cheetah was not presently in evidence, and looked round. There was only one other door, she saw with satisfaction, and turning the handle, she looked inside. It was his study. It had to be. A huge mahogany desk dominated the central area, liberally strewn with books and papers, and pushed to one side was a typewriter.

But it was not the desk itself that riveted her attention. Perched precariously on a window ledge in the corner, half concealed by heavy red velvet curtains, was a cream telephone!

Her immediate impulse was to use it to call for help, but recent events had made her wary. If she delayed long enough to make a phone call, Dominic Lyall could only become suspicious and if he came after her . . . And there was always the chance that Bolt might decide to come for the tray. If once they knew that she was aware of the presence of the telephone she would get no further chance to use it. But if she pretended she had not seen it . . .

Dragging her eyes away from that tempting link with the world outside, she moved to the desk and seated herself in the brown leather chair behind it. No wonder he had not wanted her to get his tablets for him. But obviously his ultimate need had got the better of his jugement. A remembrance of his face distorted with pain brought her hand to the handle of the top right-hand drawer. No matter how her feelings revolted at his deliberate duplicity she could not ignore his suffering.

A swift resumé of the drawer she had opened assured her that there was no bottle of tablets there, and she closed it again. The left-hand drawer seemed full of files, but pushed towards the back she found what she was searching for. A small brown bottle containing white tablets.

Casting an uncomprehending glance at the mass of papers on his desk, she closed the second drawer and rose to her feet. She had reached the door when Bolt came out of the kitchen and her knees felt weak at the thought that if she had used the telephone he would have caught her in the act.

He frowned, however, as she closed the study door and said: "Are you looking for something, miss?"

Helen could not prevent the wave of colour that washed her cheeks. She felt guilty, and it showed. She held up the small bottle. "Your employer has a migraine," she explained, walking towards the living room once more with more confidence than she felt. "I was just getting his tablets."

"I see." Bolt was genuinely concerned. "I'll get some water."

Helen made an involuntary movement of her shoulders. "If you like," she said jerkily.

Bolt went back into the kitchen and she entered the living room. Dominic was still lying on the couch with his eyes closed and she had to force herself to remember that this was the man who was holding her here against her will.

She walked to the couch and looked down at him. "Here are the tablets," she said quietly. "Bolt's getting you some water, to take with them, I suppose."

His eyes opened. They had a bruised darkness. "Thank you," he replied, levering himself into an upright position, and taking the bottle. "It's my own fault. I've been spending too many hours working."

Helen frowned, watching him unscrew the bottle and extract two tablets. "Working?" she echoed in surprise, unable to prevent herself.

His gaze flickered upward. "That's right – working. Did you think I spent my days in idleness?"

She shrugged, moving away from the couch. So close, his eyes had a disturbing penetration even in this weakened state. "I – I haven't thought about it," she answered, not quite truthfully.

The door opened and Bolt came into the room carrying a jug and a glass. He came straight to the couch and looked down at Dominic with gentle impatience. "Here you are," he said pouring water from the jug into the glass. "And then I think you ought to go to bed."

Dominic threw the tablets to the back of his throat and swallowed them with a mouthful of the water before handing the glass back to Bolt. "I don't think so," he said dryly, wiping his mouth with the back of his hand.

Bolt looked reproving. "You know you should."

Dominic cast a derisive look in Helen's direction. "What? And leave our guest to have coffee alone?"

Helen gasped indignantly, but Bolt shook his head when she would have said something. "After coffee then," he said firmly, but Dominic merely closed his eyes again as though the effort of keeping them open exhausted him.

"I'll let you know," he agreed resignedly.

Bolt sighed and spread his hands towards Helen in a helpless gesture, and she felt a ridiculous sense of alliance with him in their mutual concern for the man on the couch.

"For Christ's sake, stop making signals that I'm not

supposed to know about," snapped Dominic suddenly, as though completely aware of their silent correlation, and Bolt walked abruptly to the door.

"I'll come back in fifteen minutes," he said, and left them.

After he had gone, Helen remained where she was standing wondering why she didn't leave too. Then perhaps he would go to bed and that, after all, was the only sure cure for migraine. Thinking of him in bed brought a prickling warmth to the surface of her skin. His temporary vulnerability was dangerously appealing, and she had to force herself to remember that like the predator he kept as a pet he was ruthless and totally unpredictable. All the same, he had opened his shirt at the neck and she could see the beginnings of the hair that grew at the base of his throat and she knew the strongest desire to touch him. She would have liked to have massaged his temples with her fingertips and seen the muscles relax under her ministrations . . .

His eyes opened unexpectedly and found her eyes on him. "Sit down," he directed shortly. "I can stand it. I'm not about to lose consciousness or anything foolish like that."

Helen's eyelids hid the revealing awareness of her gaze. It was with difficulty that she moved to the armchair facing the fire and perching on its edge warmed her hands unnecessarily at the blaze. It would be as well when she could use the telephone, she thought rather shakenly. She was becoming altogether too interested in Dominic Lyall.

Thinking about the telephone brought her to the problem of when she might use it. The only safe time would seem to be after he was in bed at night, although the thought that Sheba might have the run of the house at that time was almost a deterrent.

"Aren't you going to pour the coffee?"

His quiet voice broke into her reverie and she started violently. "What? Oh – oh, yes. If you want me to." She swung round to the low table and clattered cups into saucers. The smell of the coffee was restoring, but her hand shook as she held the pot. "Cream and sugar?"

"As it is," he replied, sitting up to take the cup she held out to him. "Thank you."

Helen poured her own coffee, added sugar, and stirred it vigorously. She was intensely conscious that he was watching her and wondered what he could be thinking. Her own thoughts were easier to define, but no less disruptive to her piece of mind.

"Why did you change your mind?" he asked abruptly.

"Change my mind?" For a moment Helen was all at sea. "About what?"

"Taking coffee with me."

She drew a trembling breath. "Oh, I see." She shrugged. "It seemed – pointless to avoid any opportunity to persuade you to change your mind."

He lay back, his eyes narrowed. "Do you think you can do that?"

She put down her empty cup with jerky movements. "I don't know."

"But you're willing to try?"

She sighed. "I might hope to appeal to your – your sense of honour."

"My honour?" He shook his head. "That's a curiously

old-fashioned notion. And how do you propose to go about it? By making me feel indebted to you?"

"I don't know what you mean."

"I think you do. Your solicitude just now was almost credible."

Helen, who had been avoiding his eyes, now looked directly at him. "What a foul thing to suggest!"

He shrugged. "You act well, I'll say that for you. But I thought I'd better tell you that I'm not deceived that easily. I'd hate you to go on and get yourself into a position you might find even harder to recant."

"And what is that supposed to mean?" she demanded unsteadily.

His eyes were almost closed. "Simply that you have no need to try your feline wiles on me in the hope that I might weaken towards you –"

Helen sprang to her feet. "You – you flatter yourself!"

"No, I don't," he assured her dryly. "That's why I'm giving you fair warning. I thought it was the least I could do after the way you've . . .looked after me."

The mockery was evident and her fists clenched. She was tempted to blurt out that she knew about the telephone in his study, and that at least she wasn't a liar as he was. But she remained silent. What hurt almost unbearably was that he had somehow sensed her awareness of him and had put the wrong interpretation on it. He imagined she was contemplating using her youth and beauty to seduce him from his purpose, but nothing could be further from the truth. In fact, the knowledge that this grim, even cruel man, with his distorted body, could inspire the most

65

wanton longings inside her filled her with disgust. She didn't want to be attracted to Dominic Lyall. She didn't want to feel the pull of his disturbing personality. And most of all she didn't want to contemplate the sensuous consummation of that attraction that feeling his hard hands upon her and his lean body crushed against hers would bring . . .

"I – I think you're hateful!" she exclaimed, her lips trembling. "You – you're perverted. You've allowed the distortion of your body to distort your soul!"

His eyes opened wide, as hard as the topaz stones they resembled. "Yes, I have," he agreed harshly. "And you'd better remember it!"

Helen took one last look at him and then made for the door. She was feeling distinctly sick, and an awful nagging ache had begun behind her temples. For a short while he had seemed almost human, and she had stupidly responded to that gentler identity.

CHAPTER FOUR

HELEN spent the rest of the morning in her bedroom. Much against her will, she took the rest of her belongings out of the two suitcases and put them away in the dressing table drawers and the huge wardrobe. Some things were crushable, and although she tried to tell herself that it was pointless unpacking when she would be leaving soon somehow it didn't quite ring true.

At one o'clock Bolt came to tell her that lunch was ready. When she came downstairs a few minutes later, he opened the door of the kitchen and said: "I hope you don't mind, but I've served our lunch in here. Mr. Lyall's not having anything to eat, and I thought perhaps you'd prefer my company to no company at all."

Helen followed him into the kitchen. "Of course I would," she agreed, her shoulders hunched despondently. "But I'm not very hungry either."

Bolt made no response to this but seated her at the scrubbed wooden table and began putting vegetable tureens in front of her. Whatever it was he had prepared smelt good and she felt her appetite reviving.

It turned out to be a steak and mushroom casserole, preceded by a dish of savoury tomato soup. There was some of the fruit pie she had seen on Dominic Lyall's tray the night before to finish, and the cream Bolt poured over it was thick and yellow. To her astonishment, Helen did not find it difficult to finish what he gave her, although she refused to have any second helpings.

"That was delicious, Bolt," she exclaimed at last, as he poured them both a second cup of coffee. "You're going to make me fat if I'm not careful."

Bolt's broad features broke into a grin. "I doubt that very much," he remarked, surveying her small breasts pressing against the close-fitting contours of her sweater. "Besides, you can do with a couple of inches here and there."

Helen had to smile. She felt completely relaxed for the first time since getting up that morning. Bolt was such an undemanding companion, not like his master. . .

At the thought of Dominic Lyall some of her contentment fled. She must never forget that she was here under duress, and no matter how sympathetic her jailor, that was what he was.

Playing with the teaspoon in her saucer, she said: "Did – did your employer go to bed?"

Bolt nodded, cradling his cup in his large hands. "Yes. Over an hour ago."

Helen nodded. She ought to have left it there, but she couldn't. "What – er – what work does he do?" she asked casually.

Bolt looked down into his cup. "He's writing a book, miss."

"A book?" Helen was instantly interested. "What kind of book?"

"I really don't think I should discuss Mr. Lyall's affairs with you, miss," said Bolt, almost apologetically. "Why don't you ask him?"

Helen sighed. "Why indeed?"

Bolt put down his cup. "Let me ask you something now, miss. What happened between you this morning?"

Helen concentrated on the dregs of coffee left in the bottom of her cup. "Nothing much," she said off-handedly.

Bolt frowned. "What did you say to him?"

"What did I say to him?" demanded Helen indignantly. "I didn't actually *say* anything. I just got his damned tablets for him."

"I gather he didn't appreciate the gesture."

"That's the understatement of the year! Your employer is an absolute – boor!" she declared.

Bolt rose to his feet and began gathering their dirty dishes together. "You have to understand –" he was beginning, when she broke in on him resentfully.

"Why do I have to understand anything? Why doesn't he try and understand me – how I feel? I didn't ask to be brought here. And I certainly don't want to stay."

Bolt looked down at her compassionately. "I shouldn't like to see you hurt," he said.

"Me hurt?" exclaimed Helen angrily. "Why should you suppose that I might get hurt? I think he's rude and insolent and completely selfish! How could he possibly hurt me?"

Bolt raised his thick eyebrows. "You tell me," he said cryptically, and carried the dishes to the sink.

Although he protested, Helen insisted on helping him with the washing up, and afterwards, when everything was put away and the kitchen was bright and shining again, he said: "Mr. Lyall will probably stay in bed for the rest of the afternoon. How would you like to come outside with me and see the other animals?"

Helen looked towards the windows. The bright sun of the morning was partially obliterated and it looked as though it might snow again, but the temptation to get some fresh air was irresistible.

"I'd love to," she said simply, and he looked pleased.

"Well, do you have any boots – waterproof boots, I mean? And something warm to wear."

"I have some Wellingtons," she nodded. "I expected to be doing quite a long of walking." Her wry smile was self-derogatory. "And if you've dried my coat . . ."

"Of course. It's in the cloakroom in the hall. I hung it there this morning."

"All right." Helen walked eagerly to the door. "Just give me about five minutes, will you?"

Running up the stairs to her room, she wondered whether she ought to take this opportunity to use the phone. Bolt was busy in the kitchen, getting ready to go out, and Dominic Lyall was in bed.

But no. The prospect of spoiling the relationship she had with the burly manservant wasn't appealing and she would hate for him to catch her out in damning circumstances. It could wait until tonight. After all, nobody was going anywhere.

Downstairs again, her corduroy jeans tucked into the rubber boots, and an extra sweater to supplement the emerald green one, she retrieved her red suede coat from the hall cloakroom and saw to her relief that it had suffered no ill effects from its soaking. She tucked her hair inside the hood and went in search of Bolt.

It was a delightful afternoon, the kind of afternoon

Helen could only vaguely remember from her childhood. Since moving to London, winters had become horrible cold periods, when the pavements were filthy with slush, and cars became havens of warmth to take you from one heated building to another. It was a time to plan winter holidays in places like Jamaica and Barbados where the sun could always be relied upon to speed the winter's gloom.

But here it was different. The snow was clean and white, the air so fresh it was intoxicating. And she didn't feel the cold at all. She was young and healthy, she had just had a delicious meal, and her whole body tingled with well-being.

Bolt attended to the cows in the byre, clearing out the stalls and bringing fresh hay. Helen, who was a little dubious now of the doe-eyed beasts, did what she could to help, but she was more at home in the hen-house, bringing out the brown eggs, still warm from the nests.

She saw a sledge leaning against the wall of the outbuildings and when she pointed it out to Bolt he explained that he sometimes used it to carry feed for the animals.

"I found it in an old shed when we came here," he went on. "Probably belonged to the kids whose parents used to farm here."

Helen's eyes twinkled. "Could we use it?"

"How do you mean?" Bolt was surprised.

"Well, isn't there a slope around here somewhere that we might use it on?"

Bolt chuckled. "Go sledging, you mean."

"Yes. Could we?" Helen was very appealing as she looked up at him. "Please."

Bolt took a considering look around. Then he said, "Well, there is a slope at the side of the house. But it goes down to the stream. It's got a covering of ice on it now, of course, but it wouldn't bear anyone's weight. You'd have to avoid that."

"I'd be careful. I can steer. Oh, do let's."

Bolt finally gave in and they trudged round to the side of the building. Here the snow was pristine and untouched, and Helen found a childlike enjoyment in making footprints where none had been before.

The sledge was big enough for two, but to begin with Bolt insisted on standing at the foot of the hill, near the stream, so that she didn't have an accident. However, once it became apparent that she could handle the sledge, he agreed to join her and together they sped down the slippery slope, laughing at themselves and each other when the sledge upended at the bottom and tipped them both into the snow. The hardest part was trudging back up the hill again, and Helen's legs ached by the time Bolt decided to call it a day. They walked back to the house in easy companionship, and she realised that for the last couple of hours she had not once thought of escape.

She took a bath before the evening meal and after some hesitation dressed in a soft jersey wool hostess gown, patterned in shades of blue and green. The colour complemented the blue-green colour of her eyes, and the long skirt drew attention to the rounded curve of her hips. Although she refused to acknowledge it, her desire to look her best stemmed from Dominic Lyall's malicious taunts earlier. How she wished he might compliment her on her appear-

72

ance so that she could set him down and salve a little of her pride.

But her hopes were not realised. When she entered the living room a few minutes later she found it deserted, and she was hovering uncertainly in the middle of the floor when Bolt came in.

"Mr. Lyall is not coming down for supper," he explained apologetically, and Helen immediately wished she had not taken any trouble with her appearance. "I'll bring your meal in a couple of minutes."

Helen linked her fingers together. "Er – won't you join me, Bolt?" she asked, making an expressive gesture. "I mean – I wish you would."

Bolt looked down at his rough trousers and rolled-sleeved shirt. "Like this, miss?"

"Of course." Helen was warmly impatient. "I don't care how you look. I just don't find the idea of eating alone very appealing."

Bolt relaxed. "All right, miss. You sit down and I'll be with you directly."

Tonight he served slices of pork cooked in a sauce of onions, mushrooms, peas and carrots, and there was a chocolate meringue pie to finish. He also provided a bottle of rosé wine and they both had several glasses.

Afterwards, Helen lay back in her chair and smiled lazily at him. "You really are the most marvellous chef!" she exclaimed. "Were you a chef in the Army?"

Bolt shook his head. "No, miss. I was in the Marines."

"Were you?" Helen frowned. "I thought that was the Navy?"

"No. They're soldiers who can serve on board ship, that's all."

"I see. So how did you learn to cook?"

Bolt shrugged. "I taught myself, miss. Like I said — I'm a Jack-of-all-trades."

Helen looked into the glowing depths of the fire. "And now you work for Dominic Lyall."

"Yes."

"Did you — were you working for him before — before the accident?"

"Yes."

"So you were a mechanic for him?"

"I was."

Helen considered this. "It was a terrible accident, wasn't it?"

"Two men were killed outright," said Bolt dispassionately.

Helen nodded. "I suppose — I suppose you knew them."

"One of them was Mr. Lyall's brother."

Helen's eyes widened. "I didn't know that."

Bolt shook his head. "It wasn't widely known. He raced under another name. Not to be confused with Dominic, you see."

"How awful!" That stirring sense of compassion refused to be denied.

"Yes." Bolt put the empty wine bottle on the tray and began collecting their dirty plates. "I suppose you were still a schoolgirl at the time."

Helen sat up. "I was sixteen, I think. But my father was very keen on motor racing, and he had all the pictures — and the press reports. He was quite shattered by it."

"Weren't we all?" murmured Bolt almost inaudibly. Then: "So let's talk about something else. Tell me about London. It's years since I was there."

Helen stroked her fingers over the tapestry-covered arm of her chair. "London? It's just the same, I suppose."

"You don't sound enthusiastic."

She half smiled. "I'm not."

"Why? It's your home, isn't it?"

"It's where I live," she amended slowly.

"But you have parents, haven't you? A father at least."

"I have a father and a stepmother. The traditional stepmother!"

"Don't you like her?"

"Isabel?" She shrugged. "She's all right, I suppose. Let's say we tolerate one another."

"Does she have other children? Does your father have other children?"

"Unfortunately, no. I'm their one and only." She wrinkled her nose. "Much to Isabel's regret."

"Why?"

"Oh, it's a long story. You wouldn't be interested."

"I would."

She frowned. "Well, I was only twelve when Daddy married Isabel. It was her first marriage, his second. My mother died when I was quite young. Naturally, Isabel expected to have children, but it wasn't to be. And my father refused to adopt any." She gave a faint laugh. "I suppose I ought to feel gratified, but I don't."

"And your father runs this big company?" Bolt frowned. "Some engineering firm, isn't it?"

"Yes. Thorne Engineering. He's the managing director. He's done very well for himself considering that when Mummy died we were almost going out of business."

Bolt listened intently. "So how did he become successful?"

"He married Isabel Thorne."

"Oh, I see." Bolt nodded. "Very shrewd."

"Yes, wasn't it?" Helen gave a wry grimace. "And I was sent to boarding school until I was old enough to mix in company."

Bolt's eyes were gentle. "I'm sure your father only did what he thought was best."

"Best for whom?"

"For all of you, I guess."

"My father was – *is* an ambitious man. I think my mother was his only saving grace, and when she died . . ." Helen sighed. "He still has ambitions, only now he needs my help to achieve them."

Bolt put his head on one side. "And that's why you ran away."

"Yes."

"What did he have in mind? A man, I suppose."

Helen gave him a rueful smile. "You're very shrewd, too, aren't you?"

Bolt chuckled. "I should say it was pretty obvious. Who is he? Class or expediency?"

"A little of both, I guess. His father owns a controlling interest in a company my father would like to merge with, and his grandfather is a member of what they call the landed aristocracy."

"I see." Bolt nodded. "A formidable choice."

Helen made an involuntary gesture. "Oh, Mike's all

right. I like him. We've had some fun together. But I don't love him."

"You're very sure of that."

"Yes, I am. Bolt, I've known lots of boys — men young and not so young, but I've never met one with whom I could imagine spending the rest of my life. Besides — besides, I don't think men interest me all that much. Not — not in that way."

Bolt's eyes twinkled. "Oh, really? That's a grand assumption."

"No, it's not." She shook her head. "Oh, that wine's loosened my tongue. I'm not in the habit of unburdening myself to — to anyone."

"Then perhaps it's time you did," asserted Bolt calmly. "Don't you ever talk to your stepmother?"

"Isabel? Heavens, no! Not in the way you mean, anyway."

"Why not?"

"She wouldn't be interested. She has far too many interests of her own to bother about my affairs."

"And your father?"

"Well, I suppose he would let me talk to him, but he never listens to what I say. Particularly not if it's something he doesn't want to hear."

Bolt picked up the tray and got to his feet. "I think that's a great pity," he remarked, shaking his head.

Helen stretched luxuriously. "Did anyone ever tell you that you're a good listener?" she asked lazily.

Bolt pulled a face. "No. But I'm always prepared to listen to compliments." He walked a couple of paces.

"And now I'm going to do these dishes and then I'm off to bed. I'm tired."

"Yes, so am I," admitted Helen, stifling a yawn.

And then she remembered what she had to do!

"By the way," she said, standing up, "I – er – I haven't seen Sheba today."

"Haven't you?" Bolt looked round. "No – well, she was in the yard this morning, and she's been in Mr. Lyall's room since he went to bed."

"Does she sleep in his room?"

Bolt shook his head. "Bless you, no. I'll bring her down before I go to bed. She needs to be taken for a walk."

"She has the run of the house at night, then?"

Bolt gave her an old-fashioned look. "Now you're not thinking of making a dash for it, are you?"

Helen flushed. "No. I – I was curious, that's all."

"Well, as it happens, she sleeps in the kitchen."

"I see." Helen nodded. "She – she's rather a strange pet to have, isn't she?"

"Maybe so." Bolt shrugged. "Mr. Lyall was given her by a friend, but this chap – the one who gave her to Mr. Lyall – he's going to have her back soon, for breeding purposes."

"Oh!" Helen digested this. "Well – goodnight, then."

"Goodnight, miss."

Helen managed a smile and the manservant went out and left her. She wondered what she could do. Ought she to stay here until Bolt had been upstairs, brought the cheetah down, taken her out and then gone to bed himself? No. That was bound to arouse suspicion. Her best plan was to go up to her room and wait until the house was quiet.

The decision made, she went upstairs slowly. Now that she knew that Sheba was somewhere about she couldn't help the hairs on the back of her neck prickling, but she reached her room without incident. She took off the long dress, put on her jeans and sweater again and sat down to wait.

Her room, for all its radiator, was by no means as warm as the living room downstairs, and after a while she began to shiver. It seemed ages before she heard Bolt come upstairs for the first time and then she heard voices in a room at the other end of the landing which proved that Dominic Lyall was not asleep either.

She got to her feet and paced about the room, but she still felt cold and kicking off her shoes she pulled back the bedspread and got beneath it, huddling the thick cover up to her chin. That was much warmer and she could feel the heat from the hot water bottles Bolt had put between the sheets.

The snow gave the room an eerie illumination and she could hear the wind whistling under the eaves. It was remarkably cosy and she yawned sleepily. It had been quite an exhausting day, one way and another, and perhaps she had time to take a nap while she waited for Bolt to finish his chores and go to bed.

She closed her eyes. Bolt was really awfully nice. But she had done most of the talking that evening. He knew all about her now – even about Mike. She yawned again. Oh, well, what did it matter? It was no secret.

Her eyes felt heavier and heavier and with a sigh she

drifted off to sleep. It wasn't until daylight was filling the room that she opened her eyes again and realised, to her dismay, that it was morning.

CHAPTER FIVE

FORTUNATELY, Helen had time to wash and change her clothes before Bolt appeared with her breakfast. She would have hated for him to see that she had slept fully clothed. He might have got entirely the wrong impression. As it was, she was standing brushing her hair before the dressing table mirror, slim and attractive in cream flared tweed pants and a long-sleeved scarlet blouse, when he knocked at her door.

"Good morning," he greeted her smilingly. "Sleep well?"

Helen managed not to look as guilty as she felt. "Yes, thank you," she replied. "Did you?"

"Like a log," remarked Bolt, putting down the tray he was carrying on her bedside table. "I've made you porridge this morning – oh, and scrambled eggs."

"Marvellous." Helen nodded, glancing towards the windows. "Has it been snowing again?"

"I'm afraid so. It's not as bright as yesterday by any means. Colder, too."

"Oh, well, never mind," Helen sighed. "Shall I bring these things down to the kitchen when I've finished?"

"If you wouldn't mind."

"I'd like to." She seated herself beside the tray. "Er – how is – how is your employer this morning?"

"Much better," said Bolt, with evident satisfaction. "See you in a little while, then."

"Yes." Helen smiled and the manservant left the room.

She enjoyed her breakfast, perhaps not quite as much as the previous day, but then she had been ravenous, while this morning hunger came second to the annoyance she felt at having fallen asleep so soundly the night before. Even so, she made a good meal and then carried the empty tray down to the kitchen.

Sheba was in the hall, lying on the carpet outside Dominic Lyall's study, and she raised her head as Helen came down the stairs. The hair on the back of Helen's neck prickled at that unnerving appraisal, but the cheetah didn't move, and Helen walked quickly into the kitchen.

Bolt was not about and on impulse she put the dishes in the sink and turned on the taps. She hadn't washed dishes since leaving boarding school and it was quite a novelty squeezing washing-up liquid into the water and watching the suds form. She gathered some in her hand and blew them gently, smiling as enormous bubbles floated on the air.

"Good morning, Miss James. Am I interrupting anything?"

Helen forced herself not to react revealingly to that sardonic tone. Adopting a defiant expression, she turned and said: "Good morning, *Mr*. Lyall. You're not interrupting anything. What can I do for you?"

In denim jeans and an open-necked denim shirt he looked lean and attractive. The tight trousers accentuated the muscular length of his legs, and until he moved the limp was not evident. But even when he did, shortening the space between them, Helen found nothing to dismay her. On the contrary, the way he moved was singularly part of the man himself.

"I came to apologise," he said quietly. "I behaved rather badly yesterday, and I'm sorry."

Helen almost gasped. She had expected many things – anger, rudeness, impatience – but not this. Not him apologising to her! She wished he hadn't. She didn't want him to. It was much easier for her to hate him when he treated her with contempt.

"I – I – that's not necessary," she exclaimed ungraciously.

"I disagree." There was only a few feet between them now, and the tawny eyes were too discerning. "My only excuse is that I was – well, in some pain. Even so, I had no right to say what I did. In spite of your opinion of me, I was not always so ill-mannered."

Helen drew her hands out of the soapy water and dried them vigorously on the roller towel which hung on the door of the cold store. She was supremely conscious of his nearness and she half thought he knew it. "Well, all right. Is – is your migraine better?"

"Much better." He was supporting himself with one hand on the steel drainer and Helen's eyes were riveted somewhere between the bottom button of his shirt, and the narrow belt of the jeans that hung low on his hips.

"Good," she managed inadequately.

"There's no need for you to wash your own dishes, you know."

"I wanted to." She forced herself to look up at him. "Do – do you know where Bolt has gone?"

"Yes, I know." He was non-committal. "Why?"

She glanced round. "I just thought I might go outside

for a while. It looks as though it's going to snow again, and –"

"Can you make coffee?" Dominic interrupted her quietly, studying her embarrassed face.

Helen looked puzzled. "I – I think so."

"Good." Dominic straightened, one hand massaging his hip again. "Make us some. Please."

Helen's lips parted. "Us?" she echoed.

"Of course." He limped back to the door. "Bring it into the study when you're ready. We'll have it there."

The door closed behind him and Helen stood staring at the spot where he had been a moment before. She didn't know whether to feel honoured or indignant. She wasn't used to being given orders, but then it was in the nature of an olive branch, too. But the study! He wanted her to join him there! And what about the telephone?

She shrugged and gave a helpless look round the kitchen. She knew where the coffee was kept. She had watched Bolt make some for them the day before. And a percolator held no mysteries for her.

She found she enjoyed setting the tray with two of the brown earthenware coffee cups and saucers that Bolt had used, and she even discovered the whereabouts of the small burner which kept the jug hot. Every minute she expected Bolt to return and ask her what she thought she was doing, but he didn't, and when it was ready she opened the door and carried the tray across to the study.

Sheba had disappeared again, but her whereabouts soon became apparent when she knocked at the study door. Dominic opened the door to her and the cheetah was at his heels. However, at his order it walked out into the hall again and took up its previous position.

Dominic stood back to allow her to enter the room and as she did so she saw he had cleared a space on his desk for the tray. Her gaze flickered irresistibly towards the window ledge in the corner. There was no sign of the cream telephone and her heart skipped a beat. Had she imagined it? Or had he perceived her discovery and had it moved? And then she realised the red velvet curtains partially concealed the window ledge. They could be hiding it from view. Deliberately? She couldn't be sure.

Dominic indicated a chair he had placed on the opposite side of the desk and after she was seated he limped back to his own chair. Realising she was expected to pour the coffee, Helen busied herself with the cups, pouring a cup for him and leaving it black.

"Thank you," he said, as he took the cup and set it down before him. "I'm ready for this."

Helen didn't know how to answer him, and she made an effort to speak naturally as she said: "Bolt – Bolt told me you're writing a book."

"Did he?" The level tawny eyes made her wonder whether she had said the wrong thing again.

"Yes. But – but that was all. I mean, he wouldn't discuss it with me or anything."

"Did you ask him to?"

"Well, yes." Helen flushed. "I was interested."

Dominic tilted his head. "Why?"

"I – I think writing a book must present a tremendous challenge."

He considered this. "It rather depends on the type of book one is writing, I suppose," he said at last. "Some books must be harder to write than others."

Helen frowned. "I should think non-fiction is harder to write than a novel."

"Not necessarily." He shook his head. "If one is writing a factual account then it's simply a question of how convincingly one presents the facts. Fiction demands a whole new approach, with no preconceived assessments."

"I didn't think of it that way." Helen sipped tentatively at her coffee and found it as enjoyable as Bolt's. "And – and are you writing a novel?"

"Me?" He made a negative gesture. "No. My work is purely factual."

"About – motor racing?" she ventured warily.

"This time – yes."

She raised her dark eyebrows. "You've written other books?"

"*One* other book."

"And what was that about?"

His smile held slightly sardonic amusement. "I'm sure you're not really interested."

"Oh, I am." Helen flushed. "Honestly."

He hesitated and then pushing his cup across the desk, he said: "I wrote a biography of my father."

"Your father?" Helen was intrigued. "He was an officer in the Marines, wasn't he?"

Dominic looked impatient. "Bolt told you that, too, I presume."

"Yes, he did. But only indirectly. He was telling me that he'd been in the Army, and – well, it just slipped out." She looked appealingly at him. "You won't be angry with him, will you?"

86

Dominic sighed. "Why? What else did he tell you?"

"Nothing much." She shrugged her slim shoulders. "Tell me about your father. I am interested. Is he still alive?"

"No. He's dead." Dominic spoke dispassionately. "He died six years ago."

"About the time of your accident," she exclaimed impulsively, and then wished she hadn't when she saw the look on his face.

"About that time, yes," he agreed flatly. "May I have some more coffee before you go?"

"Of course." Helen was glad to have something to do. She had spoken without thinking and now it seemed she had destroyed the faint thread of communication which had been developing between them. "There you are." She paused, looking anxious. "Won't you go on? About your father, I mean."

Dominic said nothing for a few minutes, and she thought he wasn't going to answer her, but then he said slowly: "He commanded an assault force in the Far East during the war. He was awarded the Victoria Cross for spearheading an attack on a Japanese command post when he and his men were apparently quite hopelessly outnumbered."

"How fantastic!" Helen was impressed. "You must have felt very proud of him."

"Well, my mother did," he acceded, his lips twisting. "I'm not quite that old, and Francis was only a baby."

"I didn't mean that – that is –"

Helen felt herself colouring again, but at least the embarrassment she felt prevented her from asking the question which had sprung to her lips. Was Francis his only brother – the brother who had been killed in that fatal accident? If she had betrayed her knowledge of his brother's identity, Dominic might well have assumed that Bolt had discussed the accident with her, when in fact, on that subject he had been determinedly reticent.

Dominic finished his second cup of coffee and put his empty cup aside, drawing a file of papers towards him. It was dismissal, and Helen felt unreasonably disappointed. But she was obliged to get up and collect together the items from the tray preparatory for leaving. Dominic looked up as she clattered saucers together and she realised he was aware of her ill-concealed irritation.

"Bolt should be back soon," he remarked mildly. "There's no need for you to attend to those."

"I can manage."

Helen picked up the tray and marched to the door, but he moved with amazing agility and was there before her, his breathing quickened by the sudden exertion. Helen's eyes were drawn to the pulse vibrating at the base of his throat and the disturbing glimpse of his skin between the straining buttons of his shirt. Her eyes lowered to his hand automatically massaging his hip and she felt a terrible pounding in her ears. For a moment there was between them an almost tangible awareness and she was sure that had she moved closer to him she would have felt his undeniable response. It was an intoxicating experience and the eyes she raised to his were eloquent with the emotions she was feeling.

But his expression chilled her, bitter with a savage rejection of the emotions she had bee certain of arousing in him. He wrenched open the door abruptly and although she was sure he had been going to say something, he remained silent.

In the kitchen, Helen gave way to a shivering reaction. For a few moments there she had behaved in a totally incomprehensible fashion, and the knowledge frightened her. What was happening to her? She had only known Dominic Lyall three days, and yet in those three days he had almost completely taken over her conscious reasoning to the extent that she was now imagining a physical association between them that simply did not exist, except in her imagination ... She pressed her palms to her hot cheeks. She must get away. She must get away from here before something irrevocable happened. She closed her eyes, thanking whatever deity had prevented Dominic Lyall from acting on her stupid provocation, and almost jumped out of her skin when Bolt said concernedly:

"Hey, what's the matter? Helen, are you crying?"

Helen opened her eyes wide. "No. No, I'm not crying," she exclaimed, shaking her head to shake away the sense of foreboding she was feeling. She blinked. "Where did you come from?"

Bolt grinned. "I got back about five minutes ago. I was just hanging up my coat."

"Where have you been?"

Bolt sighed. "Actually, I've been to post some letters."

Helen stared at him. "Where?"

"Would you believe the post office?"

"Oh, of course. And naturally I couldn't be invited along."

Bolt looked at her impatiently, "No." His eyes dropped

to the tray on the table before her. "What's this? Have you been making coffee, miss?"

Helen nodded. "You called me Helen a few minutes ago. You can go on doing so, if you like. I prefer it to miss!"

Bolt shook his head. "I was concerned about you. It just – slipped out."

"Something else slipped out," murmured Helen moodily. "I happened to mention that I knew his father had been in the Army."

"So?" Bolt shrugged.

"I think he imagines we've been discussing his affairs." She sighed. "Oh, well – what are you going to do now?"

"If Mr. Lyall's had his coffee I suppose I can get on with lunch."

Helen thrust her hands into the pockets of her pants. "And what about me? What can I do?"

"What do you want to do?"

Helen's mouth turned down at the corners. "You've got to be joking!" she declared unsteadily.

"Apart from that."

"Oh, I don't know." She scuffed her toe. "Don't you ever see anyone here? I mean, don't you ever have any visitors?"

"Occasionally."

"Who?"

"Friends of Mr. Lyall's."

"Male – or female?"

"Both." Bolt tackled the coffee cups.

Helen digested this. Somehow she had thought he never had visitors. The general assumption that he was either dead or living out of the country had led her to assume that no one knew of his whereabouts. But of course he would have friends – and possibly relatives – who knew he lived here. She would have liked to have asked about his female visitors, but somehow she sensed that on that topic, as with others, Bolt would be uncommunicative.

All the same, she could not prevent the picture of him with some woman from entering her head, and she found the associations distasteful.

"I'm going to my room," she said abruptly, and Bolt looked up in surprise.

"You don't have to," he protested, drying his hands on the towel, but she shook her head and left him.

In her bedroom, she flung herself on the unmade bed and stared moodily up at the ceiling. She felt utterly depressed; everything oppressed her – this house, her circumstances, and most of all Dominic Lyall. What was it about him that disturbed her so? He wasn't handsome, he wasn't even good-looking, although she imagined some women might find his harsh features and deep-set, heavy-lidded eyes a more than adequate compensation. But his attitude towards her had almost always been derisive, and he could be painfully insolent when he chose. So why did he occupy her thoughts like this? Why wasn't she thinking of her father, of the ultimate effect this might have on him? Instead of indulging herself in this wholly unwarranted feeling of emotionalism. It wasn't natural – it wasn't normal; and she deserved to feel depressed.

She deliberately brought a picture of Mike Framley to mind. He was the man her father wanted her to marry. Young, wealthy, good-looking – he was the envy of her friends. And yet he left her cold . . . She pulled distract-edly at a strand of silky black hair, remembering the re-vulsion she had felt when he had first kissed her. His lips had been full and moist and she had felt stifled and im-patient for it to be over. After that he had kissed her many times and she supposed she had got used to it, but she never enjoyed it. Oh, what was wrong with her? she thought desperately. Why wasn't she attracted to Mike? Why did she stiffen every time he reached for her? Why did the idea of marriage with him fill her with revulsion?

She had thought it was her, that there was something lacking in her make-up, but now she was not so sure. Re-calling the way she had reacted to Dominic Lyall's near-ness caused a moist heat to dampen her flesh, and she real-ised she had felt no shrinking inside her at the prospect of the touch of his hands. She felt an overwhelming sense of impotence at the duplicity of her own body. Was she no longer in control of her emotions? Was this what people meant when they talked about a physical attrac-tion? Was that what was wrong with her? Was she be-coming infatuated with that cruel, destructive man down-stairs? It didn't seem possible, but what other explanation was there?

She jack-knifed into a sitting position. This would not do. She was becoming more and more fanciful. It must be spending so much time on her own, so much time thinking – imagining things.

She slid abruptly off the bed and went into the adjoin-ing bathroom. She felt hot and uncomfortable and deci-ded to take a bath. It would give her something to do and pass a little of the time between now and tonight when she was determined to use that telephone.

During the afternoon she went for a walk with Bolt.

Dominic Lyall ate lunch alone in his study and she had hers with the manservant in the kitchen. Afterwards, when the washing up was done, Bolt suggested they went out for a while and Helen sensed that he was trying in some part to make up for not being able to take her to the post office with him that morning. All the same, she couldn't help but wonder exactly how far to the post office it really was. If Bolt could be there and back in a little over an hour, it couldn't be that far, could it?

But when they went outside she saw tyre tracks flattening the snow leading towards the lane which she and Dominic had followed to reach the house when he had first brought her here, and she realised they must have a vehicle of some sort.

"Do you – have a car?" she enquired tentatively, as she stood just inside the cow byre watching Bolt shovelling manure from the stalls. If they did, and it seemed likely, perhaps she could use that to make her getaway. Sheba couldn't harm her if she was inside a car.

Bolt leaned on his shovel, looking across at her. "We have a Range Rover," he said amiably.

"Have you?" Helen tried to hide her elation. "I – er – I haven't seen it about."

"Probably because it's kept in a garage," remarked Bolt, returning to his task. "Have you ever driven a four-wheeled drive vehicle?"

Helen forced a light laugh. "Heavens, no. I wouldn't know how to begin," she said blithely.

Bolt seemed to believe her.

93

"It's not always easy," he said, straightening to rest his back. "Not if you're not used to it."

Helen changed the subject. She had the feeling that Bolt was trying to tell her something, but she didn't want to listen.

Afterwards he took her walking up the hill behind the house. It was, as he had said earlier, much colder, but the exercise sent the blood circulating warmly through her body. She returned to the house feeling distinctly more cheerful, although whether that was because of the walk or because of the knowledge of that Range Rover sitting patiently in its garage she could not be absolutely certain.

She wore another long dress for supper that evening. It was one of her favourites, sapphire blue velvet, with a scooped-out neckline that showed the purity of her camellia-white skin, and long sleeves that came to a point at the wrists. She looped up the wings of ebony hair at each side and secured them with a diamond clasp on the crown of her head, leaving two curling tendrils to hang beside her ears. She wore little make-up at the best of times and tonight she merely enhanced the colour of her eyes with some green eye-shadow and smoothed an amber lipstick over her soft mouth.

Dominic Lyall was in the living room when she entered, helping himself to some Scotch from the bottle beside him, and his eyes flickered over her speculatively without showing any of the admiration she had half hoped for. He did not get up either and she hovered uncertainly by the door, eyeing the cheetah on the hearth at his feet.

He routed the animal with one suede-booted foot and then said: "Sit down. You'll have to excuse me if I don't get up, but I'm afraid I find it easier to remain seated this evening."

Helen linked her fingers together and moved forward. She wished she had not taken such trouble with her appearance. She felt decidedly over-dressed, while he, in the black garb he had worn the day before, looked like a silver-haired devil.

When she was seated he poured a small measure of Scotch into a glass, added a splash of soda, and handed it to her. Helen took it because he expected her to do so, but she didn't greatly care for whisky.

"Well?" he said, his tawny eyes insolently appraising. "Is this for Bolt's benefit – or for mine?"

Helen refused to be intimidated. "I'm used to dressing for dinner," she stated coolly. "My father always says that it's good for morale."

"Does he?" Dominic inclined his head in acceptance of this. "And how is your morale this evening?"

Helen was taken aback by his question. "I – I – why do you ask?"

"Why do women invariably answer one question with another? I'm curious to know how you're enjoying your stay with us."

Helen was angry. "You must know I'm not enjoying it at all!" she exclaimed.

"On the contrary, Bolt tells me you've been walking and sledging and getting plenty of fresh air. Wasn't that what you came north for?"

"I came – north to be independent," she declared impatiently, "not to exchange one bondage for another!"

"Is it as bad as that?"

All of a sudden the mockery was gone from his voice, and that awful weakness was invading her lower limbs. She stared tremulously at him, trying to read the expression in the narrowed eyes between their thick growth of lashes. His mouth had a sensual curve as he returned her gaze and she felt her antagonism towards him melting beneath a surge of wanton longing such as she had never experienced before. The blood was rushing madly through her veins and her breathing was shallow and rapid. She wanted to go to him, to wrap her arms around him, to tell him that if he wanted her here she would never leave, but it was mindless insanity. Her lips parted and her tongue appeared, but before she could speak he rose abruptly to his feet, wincing as he jarred his leg.

He moved across the room, but his pain transmitted itself to her with almost physical perception. On impulse, she rose too and went after him. He was standing with his back to her, his knuckles supporting him on the opened lid of the bureau, and his attitude was one of such dejection that she stood behind him helplessly, and said:

"Are – are you all right?"

"Yes," he muttered, through gritted teeth, without turning. "I'm perfectly all right."

She twisted her hands together. "Are you sure? Is there anything I can get you? Is there anything you need? Are you in pain? Shall I tell Bolt?"

He swung round then, leaning back against the bureau, his lean face mirroring the self-contempt she had come to expect. "Your concern does you credit," he said harshly, and she saw he was a little paler than before. "Particularly after what I said." He drew a deep breath. "But no, Miss

James, there's nothing you can do. Thank you."

Helen was tempted to protest, but she could sense the hardening within him and knew it would be useless, and Bolt's arrival at that moment with their supper curtailed any further conversation between them.

The manservant surveyed their closeness beside the bureau with obvious curiosity, but he merely shrugged and put down the tray while he put the low table in position on the hearth. Dominic limped back to his seat and Helen did likewise, but she looked up in surprise when he said:

"Join us, Bolt. I'm sure Miss James finds your company more enjoyable than mine."

Bolt hesitated, but something seemed to pass between him and his master and with a smile, he accepted the invitation. "Thank you, sir, I'd like that."

"Good. A cosy supper for three."

Dominic stretched indolently in his chair, his injured leg resting on the wrought iron fender that surrounded the fireplace. Looking at him Helen wondered why it was that his every movement held such a sexual fascination for her, but when he caught her eyes upon him she could not read his expression.

And of course, it was not cosy at all. Helen was supremely conscious that Dominic's invitation to Bolt had been somehow stimulated by the scene that had taken place before the manservant's arrival, and she found herself in the ignominious position of feeling that he was deliberately showing her that her behaviour was nothing but an embarrassment to him. *To him*!

Helen felt sick and humiliated. What was it that possessed her so that when he looked at her in a certain way she forgot her antagonism and had no defence against him? Did he know what he was doing? Or was it an involuntary attraction? Or did some perverted streak in his nature find amusement in her stumbling naïveté?

She ate very little of the fried chicken Bolt had prepared, but fortunately the two men found plenty to talk about, to each other, and her lack of enthusiasm for the food was not commented upon.

When the meal was over, and the two men were smoking cheroots, Dominic looked across at Helen and deliberately, she thought, he said: "I think I'll do some work this evening, Bolt. I'm not tired. I rested this afternoon while you were out. I feel like burning the midnight oil."

Bolt shook his head. "So long as you don't overdo it," he commented dryly.

"Oh, I won't." Dominic stretched lazily, his eyes on Helen's suddenly frustrated face. "But if we're to leave here soon, I must get on with the book."

Helen looked down at her hands locked together in her lap. She was almost sure now that he was aware that she had seen the telephone in his study, and this was his way of warning her not to come and try to use it tonight. A choking tightness closed round her throat and her nails curled painfully into her palms. How could she ever feel anything but loathing for someone who constantly used her to gratify his own sadistic sense of humour?

CHAPTER SIX

DURING the next couple of days Helen had no opportunity to seek any means of escape. She awoke on the morning following the supper party with a throbbing head, a burning throat, and a streaming nose. When Bolt appeared with her breakfast, he insisted on taking her temperature, and after that he refused to allow her to get out of bed.

"You don't want to get pneumonia, do you?" he asked reprovingly, when she protested weakly that she couldn't put upon him in this way. "This has been coming for a few days, if you ask me – ever since the afternoon you arrived when you got soaked. You stay where you are and I'll bring you some hot water bottles. You're not fit to go downstairs and you know it."

Helen did know it. She felt terrible, and it was a great relief to abandon herself to Bolt's administrations, knowing that he would think no worse of her for giving in. She didn't want to think what Dominic Lyall's reactions might be, and as she slept for the most of that day thoughts of him did not intrude upon her aching brain.

The next morning she felt considerably better, but not strong enough to get up, and Bolt brought all her meals upstairs, dismissing her apologies with casual inconsequence. He brought her some books up, too, paperbacks mostly from the shelves in the living room, and Helen spent the day reading and sleeping and generally regaining her strength. Once or twice when she heard footsteps on the stairs she tensed, half expecting Dominic Lyall to come and see how she was, but only Bolt ever came into her bedroom.

The third morning found her almost fully recovered. She was in her dressing gown when Bolt brought her breakfast tray and smiled away his assertions that she ought not to be out of bed.

"I'm much better, really I am," she exclaimed, looking at him appealingly. "And I do want to thank you for looking after me as you have, bringing me aspirins and cough medicine and hot water bottles. I don't know how to thank you."

Bolt shook his head. "I was glad to do it, miss."

"Helen."

"All right, Helen." He grinned. "Well, I'm glad to see you're better, but I'd suggest you didn't get up until this afternoon. Give yourself a chance. You've just spent two whole days in bed."

"I'll think about it," she promised, moving over to the tray. "Hmm – mushrooms and bacon. I shall enjoy that."

After Bolt had gone about his business, Helen ate her breakfast and then wandered to the window. It was a fine morning, if a trifle overcast, but at least no more snow had fallen since she became ill. She turned to survey her bedroom and then on impulse went into the bathroom and washed and cleaned her teeth. She was tired of staying in her room, and now that she felt so much better she wanted to be up and about. She could always sit in the living room. And she would have Bolt to talk to. She refused to consider Dominic Lyall's feelings in the matter. He had not even bothered to come and ask how she was feeling. And she couldn't help that rankling a little.

She dressed in tight jeans and a cream shirt and taking her tray with her went downstairs. Bolt was not in the kitchen and she put down the tray and looked about her. It was amazing, but already this place possessed a certain familiarity for her, a feeling of association that she had never experienced in the house her father shared with Isabel.

Looping her hair behind her ears, she looked out of the kitchen windows wondering where Bolt could be. Had he gone to the shops again, or was he outside feeding the animals?

The cold storeroom door stood wide and a sound from within made her turn in surprise.

"Bolt?" she said tentatively. "Bolt, is that you?"

She went to the door of the storeroom and looked inside, and then noticed that there was another door at the far side of the storeroom, and it stood wide, too. Frowning, she moved slowly across to the second door and saw a flight of stairs leading down.

A ripple of excitement slid over her. It was like the thriller she had been reading the day before. A secret door – a hidden staircase; and beyond . . .

She began to descend the stairs. She was sure now that Bolt was at the bottom. They probably led to the cellars of the house. No doubt Bolt stored supplies down here.

At the foot of the stairs it seemed that she was right. She was standing in a cellar lit by a single bulb hanging by its cord. But Bolt was not here and as she looked around she saw another door standing slightly ajar.

With an inescapable feeling of trespass she went towards the inner door and opened it silently, stifling a gasp when she saw what lay beyond. No ordinary cellar this, but a magnificently equipped gymnasium with vaulting horses and wall bars, rings suspended from the ceiling, ropes and a punch-ball, and machines for exercising. She walked into the middle of the room looking about her in amazement, realising that this was why there was not an ounce of spare flesh on Dominic Lyall's muscular body in spite of his enforced inactivity.

At the end of the gymnasium another door opened into a kind of changing area, panelled in Swedish wood with an adjoining shower room. It was quite hot in here, the atmosphere was moist, and Helen found that she was sweating. The heat seemed to be coming from beyond another door and without giving herself time to have second thoughts she turned the handle and looked inside. A feeling of intense excitement filled her. The inner room was a sauna, lit by a dull orange light and incredibly hot. A man was lying face downward on a slab in the middle of the floor, and even as she realised it was Dominic, he said impatiently:

"For God's sake, hurry up, Bolt. I've got work to do."

Helen caught her breath. He had obviously heard the door open and assumed it was Bolt. If he turned round now and saw her ... Her cheeks flamed. She had never seen a man unclothed before, not in the flesh.

While she was hesitating about closing the door again and fleeing back to the comparative safety of the upper floors he spoke again. "Just here," he said, stretching one hand to indicate a spot on his back just below the level of his hips. "It aches!"

Helen felt her stomach contract nervously. If she didn't do something soon he could be bound to turn and see her. She ought to go. She ought to leave now while she had the chance and not risk his discovering her there. But something, something stronger than the desire to make her escape, was urging her to stay. She knew she was a fool. She knew she was inviting further humiliation, but she closed the door and advanced into the room. She had guessed Bolt was a masseur and she knew sufficiently much to believe she could emulate him for a while without discovery.

Her hands were trembling as she laid them on the small of his back and began smoothing the muscles that supported his spine. There was a moment when he stiffened and she thought he was about to turn and confront her, but then he relaxed again and her confidence strengthened her fingers. She kneaded the flesh more firmly, stimulating the circulation. The heat in the room made his skin damp and because she was fully dressed she grew even hotter. Her breathing quickened, and just when she thought she would have to give up because her arms were aching, he rolled on to his back, dragging a towel over his lower limbs.

Helen's lips parted in alarm, but his eyes showed nothing but a faint admiration. "You're good," he remarked, without a trace of embarrassment.

But Helen was embarrassed. He was decidedly too attractive in this mood, and she had enjoyed touching him too much.

"I – I – how did you know it was me?" she exclaimed.

Dominic smiled, a lazy smile that showed his even white teeth. "Bolt has a much heavier hand," he replied. "Why did you do it?"

Helen looked down at her wet hands, making an involuntary gesture. "I – I wanted to," she answered honestly.

Dominic's eyes narrowed and he sat up on the slab in one lithe easy movement. "That's a very provocative thing to say," he commented quietly.

"Is it?" Helen was glad of the orange light to hide the brilliant colour in her cheeks.

"You know it is."

Rivulets of perspiration were running down his arms and his chest, his hair was artificially darkened by the damp atmosphere. But Helen did not move away. His eyes were on a level with hers and there was none of that mockery in them that she had grown to expect. On the contrary, they had a disturbingly sensuous softness, and her throat felt suddenly dry. He put out his hand, curving it behind her neck, under the weight of her hair, his thumb probing her jawline. Still she did not move. She felt riveted to the spot.

"Oh, Helen," he groaned huskily, and propelled her face to his, his mouth moving caressingly against her cheek and around the parted softness of her mouth.

She stood in that partially stooped position, her knees trembling, waiting for the revulsion she usually felt at the touch of Mike's lips to come. But it didn't. Instead, she moved her face against his, seeking his mouth with her own, and when it finally made contact all her preconceived ideas of what kissing could be were dispelled by a force of emotion stronger than herself. Dominic's mouth

104

parted hers, it wasn't soft and moist, but hard and demanding, and the pressure of his hand on her neck increased until she stumbled against the slab and was gathered close to the lean strength of his body. Dominic swung his legs to the floor, holding her against him, his hands cupping her nape as he continued to kiss her.

"Dear God!" he muttered unevenly, lowering his mouth to the scented hollow between her breasts, visible above the open neckline of her shirt. "This is insanity!"

Helen hardly heard him. Her arms were about his neck, her hands were in the thick hair which grew low on his neck, she was beyond coherent thought in a world where only she and Dominic existed, where it was imperative that he should go on holding her and kissing her in this urgent, passionate way, making her overpoweringly conscious of his own throbbing masculinity.

His hands at last closed over her upper arms and with a supreme effort he put her away from him, getting to his feet and wrapping the towel about his hips. He raked his fingers through his hair and then limped awkwardly away from her, bearing down heavily on his uninjured leg.

Helen watched him helplessly. "Dominic . . ." she murmured questioningly. "Dominic, is something wrong?"

He cast an impatient glance at her over his shoulder. "For God's sake, Helen, you can't be that naïve! You know what's wrong!" he responded violently. "Have you any idea what you're doing to me?"

Helen licked her lips. "I – I know what you're doing to me," she ventured.

He swung round irritably. "You shouldn't have come down here," he muttered vehemently. "I shouldn't have
105

let you –" He broke off abruptly. "I think you'd better go."

Helen stared at him disbelievingly. She couldn't accept his summary dismissal. She was on fire with an emotion she only vaguely understood, but that Dominic was the instigator of that fire she had no doubt.

"Dominic –" she began again. "Please don't be angry –"

"Angry? *Angry?* Lord, how do you expect me to be?" He looked down at his injured hip and a spasm of pain crossed his face. "Helen, get out of here! Now! Before I change my mind."

Helen had made no move when the door opened and Bolt came into the room as he had that evening three days ago. This time, however, his reaction was more acute.

"Helen!" he exclaimed. "You're soaked to the skin!" He came close to her and put a hand on her forehead. "You're on fire! What in heaven's name have you been doing?" His gaze flickered to Dominic and a strange look crossed his face. "Do you want to be ill again?"

Helen dragged her gaze from Dominic's. "I'm – all right, Bolt. Really. I – er – I'm hot because of the heat in here, that's all. And I'm wet because I've been sweating."

Bolt clicked his tongue impatiently. "I suggest you go into the shower room and make use of it," he stated dryly. "If you can tell me where a change of clothes is, I'll go and get them for you."

"Really, that's not necessary –"

"On the contrary, I think it's very necessary," returned Bolt, putting down the bottle of oil he had been carrying. "You don't mind waiting a few moments longer, do you, sir?"

Dominic shook his head and turned away. Bolt took Helen's arm and drew her determinedly out of the sauna room and into the changing area. "That's the shower," he indicated, closing the sauna room door with a firmness that belied his real feelings. "Now where are your clothes?"

Helen flushed, but she could see that there was no point in trying to evade the issue. "You'll find – underclothes in the dressing table drawer. And the corduroy jeans and sweater I was wearing a few days ago are hung together in the wardrobe."

"Good." Bolt was pleased. "Now, you get that shower. I'll be back before you're finished."

It was good to take a shower again, and Helen revelled in the warm stimulating spray, but her thoughts were still with Dominic Lyall in the sauna room. She re-lived the past few minutes in intimate detail, finding a vicarious thrill in recalling the pressure of his firm mouth on hers, and the sensual hardness of his lean muscular body. She closed her eyes and felt again the surge of urgent need he aroused within her and wondered how she could ever have imagined that she was without emotion. But no man had aroused her as he had done, aroused her and yet left her with a hunger that only complete surrender to him could assuage.

Her cheeks flamed anew. Here she was, actually contemplating making love to a man who was keeping her here against her will! She must be mad! Crazy! Insane, as he had said.

She sobered. The shower was cooling and so was she. She had done it again, hadn't she? She had allowed him to catch her off guard. Or was that entirely fair? Hadn't it been wholly her fault that he had touched her? Hadn't she been the one to arouse him by the silent supplication he had felt beneath her hands?

Someone was rapping on the door, and she called: "Who is it?" rather tremulously.

"Me – Bolt! Your clothes are outside the door. I'm going to give Mr. Lyall his treatment. Can you manage alone?"

Helen answered that she could and when she emerged into the gymnasium carrying her dirty things she felt infinitely cleaner. She wondered what she ought to do with her soiled clothes. She had no washing powder, but perhaps Bolt had, and maybe she could attend to them herself. She decided to leave them in the kitchen and mention them at lunch, but when she reached the ground floor a staggering thought struck her. If Dominic was in the sauna room and Bolt was massaging his hip, the study was empty . . .

With a thumping heart she dropped her clothes in a heap in the corner and hurried out into the hall. Fortunately there was no sign of Sheba either, although she opened the study door with extra caution just in case. But the room was deserted, as she had hoped, and closing the door quietly behind her she hurried across to the window ledge where she had first seen the telephone. She dragged the curtain aside. The phone was still there and her fingers shook as she reached for it. Who should she phone? Her father in London, or the local police? No, not the police, she decided quickly. She didn't want to involve the police in this.

She put the receiver to her ear and then, with her brows drawing together in perplexity, saw the thing she had not noticed before. The cord that was attached to the base of the telephone was hanging loosely against the wall. It was not attached to anything. It had been disconnected.

She dropped the receiver as if it had burnt her and stood back aghast. She felt a tremendous sense of betrayal, out of all proportion to what had occurred. After all, Dominic had told her he did not have the use of a telephone. It was her fault that she had seen the receiver and imagined it must needs be connected. It merely proved that he had not been lying to her after all.

With hunched shoulders, she tugged the curtain back into position, hiding the cream telephone from view, and left the study. She was glad that no one had come upon her there and found her making a fool of herself. She went slowly up the stairs to her room. So the telephone was out. That particular escape route was to be denied to her. That only left the Range Rover, and she didn't even know where that was.

She couldn't bring herself to go downstairs again before lunch. She told herself it was because she was sick and dejected, but truthfully it was because she didn't feel she could face Dominic again. Not yet . . .

When she eventually did go down, it was to find Bolt in the kitchen, setting the table for two. He looked up cheerfully as she came in and said: "So there you are! I was beginning to think I would be having lunch on my own. Did you go back to bed?"

Helen shook her head. "No. I – I was resting."

"Good idea."

Bolt went on about his business and Helen fidgeted with the cutlery at her side of the table. "Is – er – is Mr. Lyall not having any lunch?"

"He's having a sandwich in his study," said Bolt, straining potatoes over the sink.

"Oh, I see." Helen felt contrarily disappointed now that she knew she would not be seeing him after all.

Bolt turned back to her. "Helen –" He paused. "Helen, don't get involved here. I'm telling you for your own good."

Helen concentrated on the scrubbed surface of the table. "I don't know what you mean."

"Yes, you do. Look, it's nothing to do with me and you can tell me to mind my own business, if you like, but I'm not blind, you know. I can guess what happened this morning."

Helen sat down rather suddenly. "Can you? Why? Has it happened before?"

Bolt gave her an impatient look. "No, it hasn't happened before. But I know Dominic pretty well by now, and – well, I just hope you had the sense to –" He broke off, obviously finding it difficult to express himself.

"He didn't seduce me, if that's what you're trying to say," said Helen flatly.

Bolt's broad features turned slightly pink. "I just don't want you to get hurt, Helen."

"You keep saying that. How am I going to get hurt?"

"By getting involved with Mr. Lyall."

"Isn't that rather disloyal?"

Bolt sighed, sinking down into the seat opposite. "Helen, let me tell you something, something very few
110

people know. Dominic blames himself for the accident – the accident that killed his brother."

Helen's eyes widened in dismay. "Why?"

Bolt hesitated. "I can't tell you. Besides, it's a long story."

"But you must tell me!" Helen rested her elbows on the table, staring at him. "Bolt, please! I want to know."

The manservant shook his head rather doubtfully. "Mr. Lyall wouldn't like it."

"Need he know?"

"And what happens when you leave here? When you return to your family? Who else will learn the truth then?"

"No one. I swear it."

Bolt made a negative gesture. "I find that hard to believe."

Helen held up her head. "I don't tell lies."

"I'm not suggesting you do. Just that you might – well, inadvertently say something at some time . . ."

"Oh, *Bolt*!" Helen cupped her face in her hands.

He studied her dejected features for several seconds and then said perceptively: "It's too late, isn't it? You're already involved."

Helen's fingers moved over her cheeks. "I don't know." She shrugged helplessly. "I don't want to be. I keep telling myself that I should hate him for keeping me here – but I don't." She grimaced. "To think when I left London I was running away from men!"

Bolt frowned. "Are you sure you're not confusing sympathy with – something else?"

Helen gave a mirthless laugh. "I don't know. I don't

know what to think. I only know that when he comes near me . . ." She halted abruptly. "Is – is his limp a permanent thing?"

"Oh, yes," Bolt nodded. "Part of his hip was shattered in the crash. The surgeons had to remove the splinters of bone."

"I see."

"At the time, when he recovered from the initial injuries, they wanted to operate again, to insert an artificial piece of bone to take the place of that which had been shattered, but Mr. Lyall wouldn't allow them to do it."

"Why not?"

"I don't know. Everyone tried to persuade him, but he wouldn't have it. It was as though he wanted a permanent reminder . . ." Bolt sighed. "Naturally it aches when he stands too long, and his spine becomes painful. That's when massage can help."

"I understand." Helen listened intently. "I know a little about such things. My mother suffered from terrible headaches and she used to like me to massage her temples and the back of her neck." She hesitated. "Oh, Bolt, won't you tell me why Dominic blames himself for the crash?"

Bolt got to his feet. "He believes his brother tried to kill himself because he'd discovered that his wife was in love with Dominic."

"What?"

Bolt made an involuntary gesture. "Francis followed in his father's footsteps and joined the Army. He met Christina when he was out in Cyprus. He got married without telling anyone and brought his wife home. She

112

was a bitch. As soon as she met Dominic – well, that's better left unsaid. Sufficient to say she persuaded Francis to leave the Army and take up motor racing as his brother had done. Francis wasn't cut out to be a driver, but that didn't matter to her, and he was infatuated enough to try anything. He had a few races, did averagely well, but that wasn't enough, of course. Dominic was winning his races, and Christina liked a winner."

Helen's mouth felt dry. "And – and Dominic?"

Bolt half smiled. "Oh, no, Dominic wasn't interested in her. And besides, she was his brother's wife."

"So – what happened?"

Bolt sighed heavily. "It was the night before the race at Nurburgring. We had all gone to Germany several days before, and we were staying at the same hotel near the track. That night Francis and Christina had a row. They were always having rows. Christina wanted Francis to take her out, but he wanted to rest. Motor racing is a gruelling sport at best, and it calls for complete physical fitness. Anyway, she eventually went out on her own and when it got late and she hadn't come back, both Dominic and Francis went to look for her. Dominic found her in some sleazy beer-garden, fighting off the attentions of a couple of sailors. She wasn't sober, of course, and Dominic had to get rid of her admirers before he could get her away. Christina put the wrong interpretation on his behaviour. He'd have done the same for any woman, but Christina didn't see it that way. When Francis came back she told him that she didn't love him, that it was Dominic she wanted. She said that Dominic felt the same, and no matter how he denied it, Francis wouldn't believe him."

"Oh, Bolt!"

"Not very pleasant, is it?"

"So what happened?"

"You know the rest. Francis skidded on the track, his vehicle went out of control, and both Dominic and Johann Barras went into him. Francis and Johann were killed — Dominic was seriously injured."

Helen digested this. Then she looked up at him. "And — and afterwards? What happened to — to Christina?"

Bolt turned away. "Oh, she came back. She still wanted Dominic, but he'd never wanted her, and then he couldn't stand the sight of her."

"She must have loved him then."

"In her own way, perhaps." Bolt began to slice the meat. "But Mr. Lyall hasn't had much time for women since the accident." He shook his head. "The tragedy had repercussions none of us could have guessed at. Colonel Lyall had a stroke when he heard of his sons' accident, and he never fully recovered. Mrs. Lyall died only a few months after her husband."

Helen gasped, "How terrible!"

Bolt turned to look at her shocked face. "So now you can appreciate why this story must not be publicised."

"Of course." Helen clasped her hands together. "But Dominic wasn't to blame for the crash, was he?"

"Of course not." Bolt's face was grim. "The track was wet, Francis's wasn't the only car to skid. It was an accident." He sighed. "But when something like that happens — when your relationship with the person concerned is at fault — it's human nature to blame yourself if something goes wrong. Mr. Lyall was too close to see it in perspect-

114

ive. And then the aftermath . . ." He turned back to his task. "I think he just wanted to opt out of society."

"And now?"

"Well, now he has his work to occupy him. He wrote an earlier book about his father, you know. It was filmed."

"He didn't tell me that." Helen was intrigued. "Was the film successful?"

"Very successful. It made a lot of money. But it didn't change Mr. Lyall's attitude."

"Do you think – anything ever will?"

Bolt set down the meat on the table. "I doubt it," he replied heavily. "That's why – well, why I felt I had to say something."

Helen looked down at her hands. "I'm not a child, you know."

"I know that. But don't build your dreams on shifting sands. Don't expect anything, and you won't be disappointed."

"That's a very cynical thing to say."

"Mr. Lyall is a cynical man, Helen. Like I said – I don't want you to get hurt."

CHAPTER SEVEN

DURING the afternoon it snowed again and Helen, standing by the kitchen window looking out on that wintry scene, wondered how long weather like this could last in this area. It seemed to have been snowing for ever and the realisation that it was only a week since she had come here seemed totally unbelievable. So much had happened to her in that short space of time that her life in London had assumed almost an unreal quality.

She turned from the window and hugging herself closely surveyed the empty kitchen. Bolt was outside attending to the animals, but he had insisted that she remained indoors. She had not objected. She felt curiously drained and lacking in energy, and while she told herself that the time she had spent in bed was responsible for this weakness, she knew it was not so. In spite of what Bolt had said, her mind revolved continually round that scene in the sauna room, and now that the telephone had proved useless there seemed no escape from the inevitability of her thoughts. She supposed she had behaved foolishly, irresponsibly, allowing physical desires to rule sanity and reason. She should be appalled that she, who had always imagined herself in control of every situation, could have exhibited such a complete lack of control in her response to Dominic Lyall's undoubtedly experienced lovemaking.

She drew an unsteady breath and paced restlessly about

the room. It had been all her doing. She had taken the initiative, she had been the one to touch his smooth skin, to use the massage in the form of a caress. But it had been an irresistible impulse and what had followed could still bring the warmth to her cheeks and turn her limbs to water. She ran her fingers round the back of her neck, under the weight of her hair, feeling muscles still tender from the pressure of his fingers. She slid a questing hand beneath her sweater and touched the spot between her breasts where he had laid his lips. She quivered. She had never felt like this before, and the deep depression she was feeling stemmed from the frustration of desires unfulfilled. She now knew what it was to want a man – but not just any man: Dominic Lyall.

She left the kitchen. She was afraid Bolt might come back and find her in this fanciful mood. Quite honestly, her feelings frightened her a little and she was ashamed of the weakness he had aroused in her. She went up the stairs to her room and flung herself on her bed, staring at the flakes of white falling beyond her window panes. She was beginning to realise that the longer she stayed here the harder it was going to be to leave when that time came. What had begun as an enforced confinement had become a bittersweet confiscation of freedom of a much more subtle kind. She was reaching the point where she did not want to leave and this knowledge brought her upright on the bed, hugging her knees, a worried frown marring her smooth forehead. What was she going to do? What could she do? And what did she want to do?

She slid off the bed and walked across to the window. She went over in her mind the things Bolt had told her before lunch, the lunch she had found so hard to eat. He knew Dominic so well, better than anyone else, she supposed, and yet even he could not know everything that had passed between them. She crossed her arms across her breasts and rubbed her palms against her shoulders. Sooner or later she would have to see Dominic again and then she would decide whether or not Bolt was speaking the truth.

She remained in her room until early evening and then bathed and dressed in a long black crêpe jersey gown that complemented the whiteness of her skin. It was a simply designed dress, but its clinging lines drew attention to every curve of her body. She left her hair loose about her shoulders and when she surveyed her appearance in the dressing table mirror before going downstairs, she was satisfied that she looked her best.

When she entered the living room a few minutes later, however, it was to find it deserted and her lips tightened. Was he to abandon her to Bolt's company once more? Was this his way of showing her that what had happened between them was not to be repeated? She stood in the centre of the floor, drawing her lower lip between her teeth, and swung round impatiently when the door opened. But it was not Bolt who stood there as she had expected, but Dominic Lyall.

This evening he was wearing a navy silk shirt and navy suede trousers, a cream fringed waistcoat hanging loosely from his shoulders. His gaze travelled almost insolently over Helen's expectant features, but she could not sustain that appraisal and when his eyes dropped lower she looked down uncomfortably at her fingernails.

His interest seemed to wane and he limped into the room closing the door behind him. He passed her, his suede-booted foot brushing the hem of her skirt as he did so. He went to stand with his back to the fire and then said: "For God's sake, stop looking at me as if you were afraid I was about to jump on you or something!"

"I'm not –" Helen spoke involuntarily, and then sighed. "How – how are you this evening?"

Dominic's eyes narrowed. "After your expert massage, you mean?"

Helen's cheeks flamed. "Don't bait me."

"So? What am I supposed to do with you?"

"You could ask how – how I was."

His lips curled. "Could I? Do you think that's necessary when you're obviously fully recovered?"

"You didn't care to come and see how I was when I was in bed!"

"Did you want me to?"

Helen bent her head. "It would have been – polite to do so."

"But you don't expect polite behaviour from me, do you? As I recall it, you find me perverted – distorted; in mind as well as body."

Helen stared at him tremulously. "That – that was in the beginning, before – before I knew you."

"You don't know me, Miss James."

Helen made an appealing gesture. "Oh, please. Can't we behave civilly to one another?"

"If you mean by that, can't we hold an impersonal conversation, then I suppose we can. What do you want to talk about?"

119

Frustration made Helen clench her fists. "You're deliberately misunderstanding me."

"On the contrary, Miss James," he said, "I understand you very well."

It was perhaps fortunate that Bolt chose that moment to join them, bringing with him the delicious aroma from the supper he had prepared. Helen was half expecting Dominic to invite the manservant to join them again as he had done before, but he didn't, and she didn't know who was the most surprised – herself or Bolt.

Throughout the meal that followed, Dominic seemed to make an effort to do as she had asked and talked desultorily about books he had read, the social scene, places he had visited, encouraging her to speak about her own life with her father and stepmother. Helen found herself telling him the things she had told Bolt, listening to the construction he placed upon her father's behaviour, beginning to understand through his eyes the inevitable loneliness her father had suffered after her mother's death which had driven him to his desire to succeed in business as a kind of palliative for her loss. No doubt he was using his own experiences to help her to understand her father's feelings and she appreciated his deeper understanding. The only thing she didn't discuss was her involvement with Michael Framley, but somehow that was taboo.

Gaining courage from his apparent softening, she said: "I suppose everyone needs an objective opinion to understand their own particular problems. I mean, in your case, for example, you were too involved to get a clear perspective of your brother's accident –"

Dominic's eyes hardened instantly. "Who told you

120

about my brother's accident? Oh, don't bother to answer. I can guess. It was Bolt. I might have known he wouldn't be able to keep his bloody mouth shut!"

Helen felt terrible: "Oh, please," she began, "don't blame Bolt. It was me. I asked questions. He – he answered me, that's all."

"He had no right to discuss my affairs with anybody."

"We didn't – discuss your affairs. Bolt merely – told me the facts."

Dominic got to his feet, wincing as the sudden movement jarred his hip. He stood for a moment looking down at her bent head and then limped slowly across the room, his whole attitude one of suppressed violence. Helen looked up as he moved away and on impulse got off her chair to kneel on the couch, looking at his broad back appealingly, willing him to rid himself of this unnecessary bitterness.

"Dominic –" she began again, and he turned to survey her with cold eyes. "Dominic, what does it matter what Bolt told me? It was all a long time ago. Why can't we talk about it?"

He stood leaning more heavily on his uninjured leg. "What gives you the right to think that I might want to talk about the accident to you?"

Helen refused to be intimidated. "I – I want to help you –"

"Really?" He limped back to the couch. "In what way can you help me?"

Helen despised herself for the feeling of coercion he was arousing in her in spite of herself. "By – by helping you to see the facts as they really are. By showing you that people are not as uncharitable as you seem to think. You have to learn to live with the world again –"

"And what if I tell you that I prefer my life as it is now? That I no longer have any desire to live in the kind of world you're talking about?"

Helen sat back on her heels, defeated. "How can you know that? You haven't tried it. I think you're afraid to do so."

She had spoken quietly, almost to herself, and she was totally unprepared for the violence it provoked. He came round the couch in one lithe movement, grasping a handful of her hair, twisting it round his fingers so that her head jerked painfully.

"What do you know about it?" he demanded cruelly. "You talk of objectivity – of understanding. What do you know of these things? What do you know of lying for months in a hospital bed, more dead than alive, wishing you *had* been the victim! Could you be objective about that? Could you understand the force that destroys one man and leaves another twisted for life –"

"You could have – had – an operation," she protested, raising a hand to her burning scalp.

"I prefer to remember," he muttered. "Besides, I don't want any filthy artificial device inside me. This hip may be distorted, but at least it's all me – not some sophisticated facsimile."

"Dominic, you're hurting me –"

"So? Be objective about it," he sneered, and her eyes widened in hurt disbelief.

"You don't mean that," she exclaimed huskily, and with a darkening of his expression he uttered a groan of self-reproach. Shaking his head, he came down on the couch beside her, close beside her, his hands capturing hers and raising their palms to his lips.

"Dear heaven," he muttered thickly, "don't look at me like that. I don't want to hurt you. But I can't help it."

Helen looked down at his bent head. The pressure of his mouth against her palm was an insistent seducement. She trembled and he looked up into her eyes, his own dark with emotion. He put his hand against her neck, his thumb moving rhythmically against the sensitive skin below her ear, and then he slid the neckline of her dress from one smooth shoulder, exposing the soft flesh to his touch.

Helen could not have moved, even if she had wanted to. His power over her was such that she would have denied him nothing. When he drew her hands to his body she fumbled so much with the fastening of his shirt that he undid the buttons for her and then gathered her close against his hard, muscular frame.

"Oh, God, Helen," he groaned against her nape. "You don't know what you're doing –"

But then his mouth was on hers, hard and firm and hungrily demanding, and she didn't much care any more. She wound her arms around his neck and somehow they were side by side on the couch, lying in each other's arms, their mouths and bodies close together, but not close enough. The kisses they were exchanging were becoming longer, more languorous, and infinitely more disturbing. An appealing lethargy was entering Helen's limbs brought on by this dangerous situation, and having the freedom to touch him at will, to caress his injured hip without rousing any response except an encouraging pressure against her fingers, brought its own weakening influence to her already inflamed senses. She could think of nothing more desirable than spending the rest of the night here, in this warm lamplit room, making love . . .

"I love you, Dominic," she whispered, beneath his mouth, but immediately he stiffened, rolling away from her on to his back, staring up at the ceiling with hardening features.

"Dominic?" she said again, propping herself up on her elbow and looking down at him. "What's wrong? I said – I love you. I do. I love you."

"Don't say such things to me," he snapped violently, swinging his legs to the floor and getting to his feet. "You don't know what you're talking about."

Helen's lips parted. "I do. *I do*! Dominic, what is it? What's wrong?"

He looked down at her coldly, thrusting his shirt back into his pants, reaching for his waistcoat and pulling it on. "I don't love you," he said distinctly. "With me, love doesn't come into it."

Helen couldn't entirely suppress the gasp that escaped her. "But – but just now –"

"I wanted to make love to you," he stated brutally. "I thought you wanted the same."

"I – I did," she breathed unsteadily.

"I wonder?" His lips twisted. "And would you have been prepared to forget all about it once this interlude is over?"

"Forget – about – it?" Helen struggled into a sitting position, dragging together the neckline of her dress. "Dominic, I – I don't believe you're – indifferent to me!"

124

He stared grimly down at her for a moment and then limped abruptly to his chair. Sitting down, he reached for the bottle of Scotch and a glass. "I wonder why it is that women can never appreciate that men can be aroused without feeling anything more than a purely animal desire to mate," he said.

Helen's face mirrored her distaste at the crudity of his words. "I – I think that's a disgusting thing to say!" she declared.

"What else would you expect from someone as perverted and distorted as me?"

"Oh, Dominic –"

"Shut up!" he muttered, raising his full glass to his lips. "I don't want to talk about it any more. I don't want to talk to you any more. You make me sick!"

Helen caught her breath on a sob. "Stop it!" she cried. "Stop saying such things! You don't mean them. I don't believe you."

His eyes narrowed. "Why not? Do you have such a high opinion of yourself? I assure you the intimacies we have just shared, I have shared with other women, and with greater satisfaction."

Helen had heard enough. She scrambled to her feet with as much dignity as she could muster and stood looking down at him with tortured eyes. "I – I think you're vile!" she got out unsteadily, "vile! I don't know how I could have imagined you were a decent man – let you touch me! I – I despise you. I despise you utterly!"

"Good." He lay back in his chair with apparent unconcern. "That's the way I like it. Now, as this is my house, do you mind getting out of this room? I intend getting stoned out of my mind!"

Helen dragged herself up the stairs to her room. She dreaded the possibility that Bolt might appear and ask her if everything was all right and she knew if he had she would have broken down in front of him. As it was, once she was safely in her room, she collapsed on the bed in an agony of weeping that did not abate for several minutes. But when at last the storm was over, she lay feeling quite bereft of all emotion.

Then she got to her feet and tore off the crêpe jersey dress. She felt she never wanted to see it again as long as she lived and she rolled it up in a ball and thrust it in the bottom of the wardrobe.

After that she stood in her long slip wondering how on earth she was going to survive another day in Dominic Lyall's house. It was useless telling herself the things she had blurted at him, that he was vile and despicable. It was useless telling herself she hated him. Because she knew it was not so. She loved him. She really loved him. And that was something harder to bear than the anger and frustration she had suffered in those first few days.

So Bolt had been right and it was up to her to do something about it. Of course, she couldn't go to Bolt for help, but there still remained the possibility of the Range Rover, and the more she thought about it, the more imperative it seemed that she should get away from here before something even more disastrous happened.

She sighed. What could happen that hadn't happened already? she asked herself, and supplied the answer. Living here with Dominic Lyall was doing strange things to her, and she was afraid that one day she would find the desire to know the forbidden fruit of sexual experience with him irresistible. And it could happen. Whatever he said, she knew he found her attractive, but his motivations lacked the sincerity of hers.

With a shake of her head she took off the long slip and searching in her drawers brought out jeans and a sweater. Once dressed again, she considered her position. It was already after ten o'clock. Bolt, she knew, would be coming to bed shortly, and if Dominic did as he said and got drunk, she would have no problems with him. That only left Sheba. Bolt had said she slept in the kitchen, so that meant she would have to leave the house by the main front door. It was unfortunate that the front door was so near to the living room, but that couldn't be helped. It was now or never, she thought fatalistically.

By eleven-thirty the house was as silent as the grave. A peep through her curtains had shown her that it was still snowing, and she stifled a sigh. What did it matter? With the amount of snow about, her tracks were bound to be visible for days.

She went quietly down the stairs and extracted her coat from the hall cloakroom. Apart from her handbag, she was taking nothing with her. As far as she was concerned the rest of her belongings could stay here.

There was a bolt as well as a lock on the front door, but fortunately the brilliance of the snow outside provided an illumination she was thankful for. The bolt slid back smoothly, the lock turned, and the door was open.

Outside, she looked about her. The night air was cold, but not frosty, and the flakes of snow fell softly on to her upturned face. With a stiffening of resolve, she moved

127

away from the front door and walked round the side of the building. She knew all the outhouses were at the back, and somehow she had to discover which was the garage.

It was easier than she had thought possible. The tyre tracks of days ago still marked the yard and she went confidently towards a barn-like building beyond the cowsheds. The double doors were not locked, merely closed and secured by a plank of wood. Panic nearly caused her to drop the plank as she lifted it out of its shafts when a sleek black body fled across the yard, but she realised in a moment that it was only one of the half-wild cats that made their home in the outbuildings.

Nevertheless, the small incident had served to unnerve her a little and she winced as the doors squeaked on their hinges. She peered inside, blinking to adjust her eyes to the darkness and then gasping as she saw that the vehicle in the barn was not the Range Rover as she had supposed but her small sports car. Until that moment she had scarcely thought about it, and if she had vaguely imagined it still buried in the snow. But now she remembered that Dominic had asked Bolt to see about shifting it, and obviously he had succeeded. She sighed. If only she had her keys! If only she knew how to connect the points to make contact possible.

Oh, well! She closed the barn doors again. It was useless anyway. The car might still be out of commission, and she could just imagine the noise she would make trying to get that useless engine started.

She looked round the yard again. There were lots of tracks now she came to study them, and they all seemed to criss-cross one another. But there was only one other building large enough to house a Range Rover and she approached it with caution.

This time she was lucky. The Range Rover stood just inside the doors, and wonder of wonders, the keys were hanging in the ignition. She could hardly believe it. Her hands trembled as she climbed inside and closed the door silently behind her. The controls looked much the same as she was used to and hunching her shoulders against the sound that igniting the engine would bring, she turned the key slowly. There was a moment when she thought it was going to fail, but then, with a touch of the accelerator, it roared to life and she knew that now she had only minutes to make her getaway.

She found a gear and the vehicle rolled forward out of the garage and onto the yard. She swung right, round the side of the house, remembering to put on her headlights in time to avoid a rain barrel, and careered across the cobbled yard at the front of the building. What was it Bolt had said about a four-wheeled drive vehicle being harder to drive? Heavens, it was easier, and the crushed wedges of snow held no fears for her. Her car would have been bogged down by now, but the Range Rover handled magnificently. She was following the tracks that Bolt must have made going to the post office and her excitement was sufficient to allay the feelings of betrayal that were rising in her. She would not think about the shock Dominic Lyall was going to get when he discovered that she was gone, or Bolt's reproachful disappointment that after everything that had happened they could still not trust her. She was escaping – that was all she was going to think about. She had achieved the impossible.

A bank of snow lay ahead of her and automatically her foot weighed heavier on the accelerator to scale it. The Range Rover bounced forward at speed, taking the bank in its stride, and picking up speed on the slope beyond. Helen felt the first twinges of alarm as she released the accelerator at once. She was going much too fast and she must slow down or she wouldn't make the next corner. She tentatively touched her foot to the brake even though she knew it was a hairy thing to do. The vehicle slewed sideways in a semi-circle and trying not to panic she drove into the skid. But the road was so narrow with its heavy drifts of snow that the rear end of the Range Rover hit a frozen mass and swung back across the road again. Her tongue protruding from her lips in her concentration not to panic, Helen again steered into the skid. The Range Rover's wheels slipped sideways and again she hit the opposite bank of snow. It was a terrifying experience, particularly as she was still moving at speed down the lane, rocking from side to side. She saw the corner up ahead of her and tried to swing the wheel, but she was out of control and the Range Rover ploughed into the mass ahead, throwing her forward to hit her head hard against the steering wheel . . .

When she opened her eyes she was lying on the road and a voice she had thought never to hear again was saying: "Helen! Helen, for God's sake, are you all right?"

Her eyes focussed on the man kneeling beside her, on the thick swathe of silvery fair hair falling across his forehead, the dark, deeply engraved features, the strange tawny eyes, curiously concerned now as he looked down at her.

"Dominic," she murmured faintly. "Oh, Dominic, I crashed!"

"I know." There were harsh lines of strain beside his mouth. "Little fool! You could have been killed!"

"Would you have cared?" she whispered, blinking rapidly.

"Yes, I would have cared," he muttered, and rose abruptly to his feet.

As he stood looking impatiently up the road, Helen gingerly lifted her head. But apart from a thumping headache there didn't appear to be anything wrong with her, and she sat upright, brushing the snow from her shoulders.

Dominic turned to look at her. "Stay where you are!" he ordered. "Bolt will be along presently with the tractor. He can pull the Rover out of the ditch."

Ignoring his command, Helen got unsteadily to her feet and Dominic turned to her irritably. "I told you to stay where you were," he muttered, and her shoulders straightened in an attempt at defiance.

"You can't give me orders," she protested. "I'm not Bolt!"

Dominic's expression was brooding. "I had noticed. Bolt isn't half the nuisance you are."

"I'm sorry."

Helen was rapidly losing what little composure she had. It had all been too much for her – his cruel indictment of her this evening, the tension that escaping from the house had brought, and now this crash and the miserable ending to all her hopes seemed the last straw. Her shoulders sagged and she felt tears rolling helplessly down her cheeks. She had never felt so wretched.

Dominic heard a stifled sob and turned to look at her. His eyes narrowed as they took in the pitiful picture she made, snow still clinging to her clothes and her hair, and an utterly defeated expression on her face.

"Oh, Helen!" he exclaimed impatiently, and before she realised what he was about to do, he had swung her up into his arms and begun walking up the road towards the house.

Helen's arms were about his neck, her head was pillowed against his chest, and she felt a sweet warmth welling up inside her. But then she remembered his hip and said anxiously: "Please – put me down! I – I can walk. You – you shouldn't be carrying me."

"I'm not completely helpless," he remarked, his jaw taut, and although she tried to get him to look at her, he wouldn't. Helen submitted and gave herself up to the pure delight of just being in his arms and for several minutes they went on in silence.

They had topped the rise which had been the start of Helen's troubles when she heard the sound of a tractor and turning her head she saw Bolt driving towards them. He stopped just ahead of them and swung down, his face eloquent of his disapproval.

"I've been as quick as I could!" he exclaimed, shaking his head. "Give her to me. Is she badly hurt?"

"I'm all right, Bolt, really." Helen raised her head, but she realised that most of Bolt's concern was for his employer.

Dominic allowed Bolt to take his burden and Helen

felt rather like an unwanted parcel.

"If you'll put me down, I can walk," she protested again, but no one took any notice of her. They walked the few yards back to the house and Helen was made overwhelmingly aware that Dominic's limp was now markedly pronounced and that Bolt somehow blamed her for it. And it was her fault, after all, she thought miserably.

There was a certain anti-climax about re-entering the building and Bolt set her on her feet in the hall and said: "Go along up to bed, miss. I'll fetch you a hot drink in a few minutes."

"That's not necessary —" she was beginning, but she was talking to herself. Dominic had limped into the living room and Bolt had followed him, closing the door on Helen with a firmness that was almost a physical reproof. She looked up the stairs, tears coming to her eyes again. They were clearly not concerned that she might make another attempt to escape tonight, and who could blame them? Besides, she felt so shattered that she doubted if she would ever be able to summon up enough enthusiasm to ever try such a thing again.

CHAPTER EIGHT

HELEN wasn't aware whether Bolt came up with a hot drink or not. Exhaustion closed her eyes almost as soon as her head touched the pillow and she didn't know another thing until a watery sun was pressing faint rays through the curtains drawn across her windows. She propped herself up on her elbows expecting to have a hangover from the headache of the night before, but she hadn't. And when she went to examine her forehead she found only a grazed bruise to signify the bump she had sustained, and her hair would conceal that.

She bathed and dressed in a short green pleated skirt and lemon shirt and was brushing her hair before the dressing table mirror when Bolt arrived with her breakfast tray.

"Mr. Lyall wants to see you, miss," he told her, as he set down the tray, and there was none of the usual warmth in his voice which she had come to expect from him.

"Do you know why?" she asked.

Bolt shook his head. "Mr. Lyall will explain when you see him, miss," he replied, and walked towards the door.

"Bolt!" Helen went after him. "Bolt, what's wrong? You're surely not – angry with me – for trying to get away?"

"No, miss."

"You are angry." Helen sighed. "Bolt, you said yesterday you didn't want to see me hurt. Surely you realise that the longer I stay here the more likely that possibility will be?"

"Yes, miss."

"Oh, Bolt, please! Try to understand –"

"I do understand, miss."

"So why are you – like this?" Her brows knit together. "Unless – unless you're sorry I didn't succeed?"

"Yes, miss."

Helen gasped. "You are? I mean – you wanted me to go?"

"It would have been the best thing."

"And you guessed I'd try," she murmured wonderingly. "It was you who left the keys in the ignition."

Bolt shrugged. "There are no thieves around here, miss. The keys are usually left in the ignition."

"Even so . . ." Helen shook her head. "I – I didn't realise you felt that strongly about it."

Bolt's jaw tightened. "You're doing no good here, miss. No good to anybody."

And with this cryptic comment, he left her.

Helen sat down to her breakfast with a heavy heart. For a week now, Bolt had been her shield against Dominic's indifference, her friend in spite of their unique positions. And now it seemed even his friendship was to be denied her. And what did Dominic want? What possible reason could he have for sending for her unless it was to issue some new punishment for last night's ill doings.

She examined the contents of the tray. Cereal, ham and eggs, toast and marmalade; they might as well have been sawdust for all the interest she had in them.

135

The idea of eating anything made her feel physically sick, but she did manage to drink a cup of coffee to calm her nerves.

When she eventually carried the tray downstairs she couldn't help but be relieved that Bolt was not in the kitchen. She quickly scraped her untouched food into the waste disposal and switched on, glad that Bolt was not there to see it. As she waited for the machine to do its work she noticed a neat pile of clothes laid on a chair. They were the things she had taken off the previous day after that scene in the sauna room, expertly laundered and ironed, and waiting for her. A lump rose in her throat. She felt hopelessly emotional. How could she go and face Dominic Lyall like this?

Calming herself, she left the kitchen and crossed the hall to the living room. Opening the door tentatively, she peered inside, but Dominic was not there. Of course, no doubt he was working in his study at this hour. She knocked at the study door, but there was no reply. A look inside assured her that he was not there either. A frown crossed her pale face. Where could he be?

"Mr. Lyall's in bed, miss." Bolt was standing on the stairs. "If I'd known you'd finished your breakfast, I'd have come along to get you."

Helen's lips parted. "Is – is he ill?"

Bolt turned. "Come this way, miss."

They went back upstairs and turned left towards Dominic's rooms. Bolt opened a door and ushered her inside and she found herself in an austere bedroom, as unlike her own as it was possible to be. The floor was polished wood, with only a couple of rugs for adornment, and the plain walls were bare. The bed was like the one in her room, but with a plain beige woven spread, and cool air issued from open windows. But although these things registered, Helen's eyes were irresistibly drawn to the man in the bed, propped on pillows, his dark face pale and drawn, a navy silk dressing gown visible above the bedclothes.

His gaze flickered over her to Bolt. "All right, Bolt," he said. "You can leave us."

"Yes, sir."

Bolt withdrew and Dominic returned his attention to Helen. "You must be wondering why I've had you brought here," he said quietly.

Helen's fingers curled into her palms. "Why are you in bed?" she burst out. "Is your hip very bad?"

Dominic's expression hardened. "Shall we leave my condition out of this?" he remarked harshly. "You're here because I've decided to let you go."

"To – to let me go!" Helen was astounded and looked it.

"That's right. Bolt has serviced your car and it's now in perfect working order. He's presently packing your cases in readiness for your departure."

Helen couldn't take it in. "But – but – what about you? I mean, are you ready to leave, too?"

Dominic shook his head. "I think not. We'll have to trust you not to reveal our whereabouts."

Helen licked her dry lips. Oh, God, she thought despairingly, she didn't want to go! Not now – with him here, in bed.

"What's wrong? Why are you in bed?" she exclaimed

again. "Please, I want to know."

Dominic's lips thinned. "Why? Does it give you satisfaction to see how weak I am?"

"You're not weak –"

"Puerile, then. What does it matter? You'll soon forget all about me and my stupid ailments." His fingers clenched round the sheet.

"I won't." The words were torn from her. "Dominic, I –"

"Please leave." His voice was cold and final. "Goodbye. With the instructions Bolt will give you, you should have no difficulty in reaching the main road."

Helen twisted her hands together. "I won't leave if you don't want me to," she whispered piteously.

But he was completely ruthless. "My dear girl, I never wanted you here in the first place!"

Bolt was coming out of her bedroom as she walked blindly along the landing. He had her suitcases in his hands and she thought that for a brief moment she glimpsed something like sympathy in his eyes. But then it was gone again and he was indicating that she should precede him down the stairs.

"I've got everything," he said, in that expressionless voice he had used earlier. "Will you get your coat, or shall I?"

"I – I will." Helen opened the cloakroom door. "Oh, and there were some things I was going to thank you for attending to –"

"From the kitchen? They're in the case, miss. Is that all?"

Helen nodded and she had perforce to accompany him

138

outside. Her car had been brought to the door, and she saw that he had taken the trouble to sluice it clean for her. He bent and put her cases in the boot and then handed her the key.

"The other key is in the ignition," he explained, thrusting his hands into his trousers' pockets. "Are you ready?"

Helen nodded again. She didn't trust herself to speak.

"Right." Bolt took out one hand and pointed in the direction she had taken the night before. "Follow that lane for about a mile and a half and you'll see a turning off to your left. Take it and you'll come to a village. That's Hawksmere. If you ask there, they'll put you on the right road for wherever you want to go."

Helen nodded once more. "Thank you," she managed chokily.

Bolt made a dismissive gesture. "It's nothing. Goodbye, miss."

"Goodbye."

Helen took one last look at the house and then at the man standing by the door and without another word climbed into the driving seat, started the engine and drove away without looking back.

She reached Hawksmere before she was able to think coherently. The postmaster there directed her to the motorway, and she drove automatically, refusing to allow her aching brain to think of anything but her immediate problems. She was driving back to London, that much was certain. Any idea she might have had about spending several weeks in the Lake District no longer appealed to her, and even the house in Barbary Square which her father shared with Isabel offered a haven to her bruised emotions.

She didn't bother stopping for lunch on the way south. She wasn't hungry, and as the road opened up before her and the weather improved the further south she came, she put down her foot and the car sped over the ground.

It was a little after two when she drove into the Square and saw her father's grey Mercedes parked before their town house. Her nerves tightened. This was something else she had to face and she had the feeling that it wasn't going to be easy.

She drew up behind the Mercedes and climbed out, her limbs stiffened after four hours' solid motoring. She had a headache, too, but that was nothing to do with driving. It was pure nervous tension.

She locked her door and climbed the steps to the house, letting herself in with her key. The sound of the door opening brought a small dark woman into the hall and she threw up her hands in surprise when she saw Helen.

"Oh – oh, Miss Helen!" she exclaimed. "Oh, Miss Helen, thank goodness you've come home!"

Helen closed the outer door and leaned back against it for a moment, summoning all her small reserves of strength. "Hello, Bessie," she greeted her father's house-keeper quietly. "Has there been a panic?"

"A panic!" Bessie came towards her shaking her head. "Oh, miss, where have you been?"

"Good God! *Helen!*"

Helen looked up at the sound of her father's voice. He was descending the stairs at speed, staring at her as if he couldn't believe his eyes. She felt a twinge of shame when

140

she saw the haggard lines around his eyes, and then she was swept into his arms and hugged close against his broad chest.

"Oh, thank God, thank God!" he was murmuring, disregarding Bessie's presence entirely. "Where on earth have you been, you independent little fool!"

Helen felt the tears hovering behind her eyes, but they must not be shed. If her father thought she was crying because of seeing him, the little advantage she had gained would be lost for ever.

"Didn't you get my note?" she protested at last, as he held her at arm's length, staring at her as if he couldn't bear not to do so.

"Note? Your note? Of course I got your note. If I hadn't I'd have been half out of my mind by now. In God's name, where have you been? I've had half the private detective force in Britain looking for you!"

Helen managed a smile. "Have you?"

"Yes, I damn well have. And I've driven Isabel almost mad with it all. Where the devil have you been?"

Helen released herself from his hands and glanced apologetically towards Bessie. "Do you think I could have some tea, Bessie?" she requested appealingly. "I haven't had a thing since – since early this morning."

"Of course you can." Bessie looked to Philip James for approval, and when it was given in the form of a brief nod, she hurried away. Then Helen's father led the way into the library, and closed the double panelled doors behind them.

"Now," he said, when she was seated in a comfortable armchair, "I want to know all about it."

141

Helen sighed, looking down at her hands. "Well – really, there's not much to tell."

"What's that supposed to mean?"

She shrugged. "I – I went to the Lake District."

"You did what?"

"You heard me, Daddy. I went to the Lake District. To – to that little hotel at Bowness where we used to stay when I was a child."

Philip James's eyes narrowed, and a frown came to mar his smooth forehead. "The Black Bull?"

"You remember it!" Helen forced an enthusiasm she was far from feeling. "Oh, we had some good times there, didn't we?"

Her father got up from the armchair he had placed opposite hers and walked impatiently across to the screened fireplace. Then he turned to look at her, one foot resting on the raised stone fender. "And you stayed there all this time?" he stated quietly.

"That's right." Helen uncrossed her fingers. "I expect it was the last place you'd think of looking for me."

"Indeed. The last place." He drew out a cigarette case and extracting a cigarette placed it between his lips. "And what did you hope to achieve by running away?"

Helen relaxed. It was going to be all right. Easier than she had thought, really. Her father was going to be angry with her, of course, once his initial relief at seeing her safe again had worn off, but she was confident she could handle it.

She looked at him affectionately. He wasn't so bad really, not deep down. And after the traumatic experience of this past week the problems she might have to face with him seemed trivial by comparison. A stirring of remembered agony brought a sudden devastating feeling of hopelessness and she tightened her lips and tried hard to think of what her father had asked her and nothing else.

"I – I needed time to think, Daddy," she said at last. "Time to be – on my own. To think things out for myself."

Philip James removed his foot from the fender and straightened. He was a man of medium height, but his stocky build made him appear taller than he actually was. "So," he said slowly, "I presume this conversation is indirectly to do with young Framley."

Helen shrugged. "In a way, I suppose."

"You still insist that you don't want to marry him?"

"Yes."

"So who the hell have you been with?" her father demanded fiercely, "because I'll tell you something, Helen – you have *not* been staying at the Black Bull at Bowness!"

Helen was lucky that Bessie came in at that moment with the tea trolley. With the familiarity of long service, she bustled about, setting out cups and saucers, drawing attention to the plate of sandwiches and the mouth-watering toasted scones and newly baked spice cake.

"I thought you'd probably be hungry, miss," she explained warmly. "You tuck in. You look proper starved, you do. Hotel or no hotel, they haven't been feeding you properly –"

"Have you been listening at the door, Bessie?" exclaimed Philip James angrily, and the little housekeeper bristled.

143

"No, I have not, sir. I don't go in for eavesdropping. But can I help it if I hear you saying that Miss Helen hasn't been staying at some hotel or other?"

"That will do, Bessie." Philip James shook his head resignedly. "You can go. Miss Helen can attend to her own needs."

The housekeeper tossed her head and left them and after she had gone Helen bent over the teapot, trying desperately not to show that she was shocked by what her father had said.

"I'm waiting, Helen." Her father resumed his seat in the armchair opposite, pressing out his half-smoked cigarette. "I want to know where you've been."

Helen hunched her shoulders. "How do you know I haven't been to Bowness?" she asked, playing for time.

"By the obvious methods. Inquiries were made. You were not registered."

"But how did you know that I might – go there?"

"I didn't. But when it became obvious that you hadn't left England, at least, not by the usual routes, I had to apply myself to the question as to where you might be."

"But – Bowness!"

"Why not? We did have some good times there. I grant you that. It was an obvious possibility."

Helen moved her head slowly from side to side. So, if she had gone to the little hotel which had seemed such a haven a week ago, her father would have found her in a couple of days. It was incredible. She ought to have known that someone so astute in business would not be thwarted by a mere girl! She should have realised that and done something completely illogical. But then she would never

144

have met Dominic Lyall, never fallen in love with him, and never suffered such pain and humiliation at his hands . . .

The feeling of hopelessness deepened. Would she have wanted that? Never to know him? Never to share for a little time at least the lonely anguish of his isolation?

No. It had had to be. And now she was to know a similar anguish of her own!

"It seems a great pity to me," she said, with feeling, "that I can't go away for a few days on my own without you hiring a gang of detectives to look for me. What did *you* hope to achieve by finding me? What would you have done if you had found me at the Black Bull?"

Her father's nostrils flared. "Don't tempt me to demonstrate, Helen," he retorted, his patience slipping. "Now, I've asked you where you were and who you've been with. Are you going to answer me?"

Helen looked up, her long eyes slanted. "And if I say no?"

Her father got to his feet. It was as if sitting still irritated him. "Helen, for the last time –"

"I haven't – *been* – with anybody."

"Do you expect me to believe that?"

"It doesn't really matter what you believe, does it?"

"Helen, I warn you –"

"Oh, Daddy, please! Can't I even have a cup of tea without this inquisition?"

Her father thrust his hands into his trousers' pockets. "All right, all right," he agreed, forcing himself to remain controlled with obvious difficulty. "All right. Have your tea. I can wait."

Helen poured tea, added milk, and then sipped the

liquid slowly. There was something enormously revitalising about a hot cup of tea and she soon finished it and poured another. She was conscious of her father standing watching her. She could feel his antagonism growing stronger by the minute. She knew he would have liked to have hauled her out of the chair and shaken her until she gave in and told him where she had been. But she was not a child any more and such tactics did not work with her. He already knew that. She possessed too much of his own stubbornness and determination.

The food on the trolley did not appeal to her. She was empty, it was true. But it was an emptiness of the spirit rather than the body. The image of Dominic as she had last seen him, pale and drawn against his pillows, haunted her, and now that she did not have the concentration of driving to distract her she felt lost and despairing. She was desperately concerned about him, and the knowledge that he had denied any further contact between them was a shattering reality.

"Well, Helen? Are you going to tell me where you've been?"

Her father's voice brought her back to an awareness of her immediate surroundings. Helen looked up at him reluctantly.

"I don't want to argue with you, Daddy," she said quietly. "Can't you just accept that I've – well, spent a few days on my own?"

"And where did you spend those few days? At a hotel?"

Helen hesitated. "Where else?"

"That's what I'm asking you."

She sighed. "I'd rather not discuss it, if you don't

146

mind –"

"If I don't mind!" Her father's fists clenched. "Helen, explanations have to be made. Not just to me, but to the force of detectives I've hired to find you. What am I supposed to tell them?"

"Couldn't you just say that it was all a terrible mistake? That I wasn't missing at all? I mean, you had my note –"

"Do you think I showed them that?" her father scowled. "What do you take me for – a fool?"

Helen put down her empty cup. "Well, I'm sorry, Daddy, but you'll have to think of something. I don't want to talk about it."

"Why not? What happened? Helen, I may not be very astute where you're concerned, but I do know when you're putting on an act. Something's upset you – or someone! And I mean to get to the bottom of it." His eyes narrowed. "What's that bruise on your forehead? How did that happen?"

Helen touched the graze with tentative fingers. "It's nothing. I bumped my head, that's all."

"How did you bump your head?"

"How does anyone bump their heads? Oh, Daddy, please! I'm tired and weary. Couldn't I just go to my room?"

"Did somebody hit you? Is that what happened? Because I warn you, Helen, if that's what did happen, and I find out who it was –"

"Don't be so dramatic, Daddy. Look, you knew how I felt about Mike before I went away. I won't be manoeuvred into this marriage, I won't. And nothing you can say can make me!"

147

Her father paced irritably before her. "And why not? What's wrong with Michael? My God, you've spent enough time with him. I thought you were fond of one another, and so did his father."

"We were – we are, I suppose. But Daddy, being fond of someone is not sufficient grounds for marriage –"

"Why not? You don't suppose Isabel and I –"

"What Isabel and you choose to do is your own affair. I want no part of it."

"Now wait a minute." Her father's face was growing red. "If you don't want to marry Michael it must be because you've found somebody else."

"Oh, really, Daddy!"

"Well? What's wrong with that?"

"Who else am I supposed to have met, with you and Mike's father breathing down our necks every minute of the day?"

Philip sniffed. "I don't know. You could have managed it somehow."

"Well, I didn't."

He looked at her squarely. "And you can tell me honestly that you've spent these last few days alone – or at least, without the company of a man?"

Helen bent her head quickly so that he should not see her face. "Yes."

"I don't believe you. I didn't believe you before, and by God! I don't believe you now. Helen, if you're lying to me –"

"What is going on here?"

The cool languid tones of Helen's stepmother were like drops of water on the heated air. For once Helen was

148

inestimably glad to see her, although Isabel's next words were hardly welcoming.

"So you're back," she observed dryly. "I might have known. Well, Philip, is this any way to greet the prodigal lamb?"

Philip hunched his broad shoulders as he looked at his wife. "Keep out of this, Isabel," he grunted. "You're back early, aren't you? Didn't you get a game?"

"Your solicitude is overwhelming, darling, but it was too cold. Keen as I am, golf is not a game to be played with freezing fingers." She cast a speculative glance in Helen's direction. "Well, and where have you been? Spending a crafty week with the gamekeeper?"

"*Isabel!*"

Her husband's voice silenced her and Helen got unsteadily to her feet. "May I go to my room, Daddy?" she requested quietly.

Philip James made an angry gesture. "Oh, yes – yes! Go! But don't think you've heard the last of this."

"No, Daddy."

Helen walked to the door with as much composure as she could muster. It was all coming back to her. The cut-and-thrust world she had been brought up in was taking over, and she hated the artificiality of it all. Maybe Dominic was right to opt out. Maybe she should do the same. One thing was certain – nothing would ever be quite the same again.

During the next couple of weeks, Helen tried to take up the strings of her old life. Her friends, learning she was back, were eager to invite her to dinner or to parties, but she had lost all enthusiasm for such outings. Even so, she made the effort. She wanted to feel at peace with herself again. She wanted to put all thoughts of that week in the Lake District out of her mind – but it was impossible. Dominic dominated her thoughts. She ate hardly enough to keep a bird alive, and she slept badly, and gradually the strain began to show.

It was Michael Framley who first noticed the change in her.

She had begun seeing him again, partly because both he and her father seemed to expect it, and partly because Mike himself was such an undemanding companion. He must have been just as curious to know the reasons for her disappearance as her father had been, but he was considerate enough not to ask the inevitable questions and Helen thought that one day she might tell him what had happened. She could talk to Mike; but whether he would show his usual understanding when it came to such a personal matter she had her doubts.

One afternoon, after he had taken her to an exhibition of art at the Hayward Gallery, they had tea at a small restaurant just off the Embankment. It was quite a warm afternoon for early March, and there were daffodils showing yellow heads in the gardens outside.

Mike waited until the waitress had brought their tea and scones and then he said quietly: "How much longer do you think you can go on, Helen?"

Helen's head jerked up. She had been idly tracing the pattern of the tablecloth with her fingernail, and had hardly been aware of his presence. "I – what do you mean?" she exclaimed, colouring.

"I think you know what I mean," replied Mike, taking the initiative and pouring the tea himself. "How long do you think you can go on living on your nerves? You don't eat – and from the look of you you don't sleep much either."

"Do I look such a hag?" she parried, with an attempt at lightness.

Mike sighed. "You don't look a hag at all, and you know it. But you and I know one another quite well, Helen, and I know that something – or someone – is eating you up."

Helen reached for her tea. "It's been a long winter."

"Has it? I hadn't noticed."

"No, well, you have your work, haven't you?"

"All right." Mike began to drink his own tea. "If you'd rather not talk about it . . ."

Helen rested her elbows on the table, cupping her chin in her hands. "I didn't say that, exactly."

"So you admit – something is wrong?"

Helen nodded slowly. "I suppose so."

"It's a man, isn't it?" Mike's mouth was drawn down at the corners.

"Sort of." Helen didn't quite know how to answer him. "Mike, you know that Daddy – I mean, you know our parents expect us to get married, don't you?"

"Of course."

"And you've guessed – at least, you must know that I – well, that I don't want to marry you."

Mike inclined his head. "It's pretty obvious even to me."

"Oh, Mike!" Helen looked at him regretfully. "You're

so – nice! I wish I did love you. How much simpler life would be."

Mike shook his head. "Life is seldom simple, Helen. And I'm sure that's just a euphemistic way of letting me down."

"Perhaps it is." Helen put her hand over his on the table. "But you are nice – and kind – and understanding."

"What a shattering submission!" Mike grimaced.

"You know what I mean."

"I'm afraid I do. In other words, I don't turn you on. But someone else does, is that what you're trying to say?"

Helen looked down at his slim white hand, so different from Dominic's hard brown fingers. "Yes," she said at last. "That's what I'm trying to say."

"So that week you were away – you were with this man?"

"I – met him while I was away," Helen amended quietly.

"I see." Mike frowned. "And your father doesn't want you to have anything to do with him, is that it?"

"Heavens, no! Nothing like that." Helen withdrew her fingers, clenching her hands tightly together. "My father knows nothing about it. And I don't want you to tell him."

"Why not?"

"Because – oh, because he would never understand."

"Why? Who is this man? What do you know about him? Where does he live?"

"Oh, Mike, please." Helen shook her head. "You're beginning to sound just like Daddy."

"All right." Mike curbed his impatience. "Suppose you

tell me in your own words."

"Well – he's an author."

"A novelist?"

"Not exactly. He writes – non-fiction."

"Do I know him?"

"I shouldn't think so."

"Why not? I know quite a lot of writers –"

"He doesn't – mix in society."

"So who is he?"

"I can't tell you that."

"Why not, for heaven's sake? Helen, you know that whatever you tell me, I'll keep in confidence, or you wouldn't have begun this in the first place."

"I know. But this is different. I – I sort of gave my word."

Mike threw himself back in his chair. "*Impasse,*" he remarked dryly.

Helen lifted her cup, cradling it in her hands. "Well, at least you know the situation."

"Do I? You say you met some man while you were away – that he turns you on! What do you mean by that? Are you in love with him?"

Helen hesitated, pressing her lips tightly together. "And if I am?"

Mike made an impatient gesture. "So why don't you get together?"

"This may come as something of a surprise, Mike, but I don't think he – likes me very much."

Mike's face mirrored his astonishment. "Helen, this gets crazier by the minute!"

"Why?"

"Well, how can you have fallen in love with this guy if he doesn't even like you?"

"Quite easily, I'm afraid." Helen sounded regretful.

"Oh, Helen!" Mike reached for her wrist. "Helen, don't you think this is all a little fanciful? I mean – okay, so you met some man you found attractive, and you imagine you've fallen in love with him. Well, it seems it's over now, doesn't it? So what can you do about it? There's no sense in risking your health by not eating and not sleeping –"

"Do you think I haven't told myself that a hundred times?" she exclaimed.

"Besides," went on Mike insistently, "he's probably married, or something. Have you thought of that? In any case, there's bound to be some woman in the picture –"

"He's not married," stated Helen firmly.

"Engaged, then."

"No!"

"How can you be sure?"

"Because I stayed at his house!"

As soon as the words were uttered Helen wished she could withdraw them. Mike was staring at her as if he'd never seen her before and the hot colour stained her cheeks.

"You stayed at his house?" Mike echoed disbelievingly. "How the hell could you do that?"

Helen shook her head. "Oh, Mike, don't ask me, please, don't ask me."

"Did you live with him?"

"If you mean by that, did I sleep with him – then no!"

Mike looked somewhat relieved. Then he went on: "But you did have some kind of relationship with him,

154

didn't you?"

"You might say that."

"Oh, Helen!" He breathed deeply. "Helen, why won't you tell me the truth? I – I might be able to help you."

Helen finished her tea and pushed the cup aside, refusing his offer of a second. "All right," she said slowly. "I'll tell you as much as I can." Mike nodded, and she continued: "Well, my – my car broke down in the blizzard –"

"What blizzard?"

"The blizzard I drove into."

"So you did go to the Lake District?"

"Yes." Helen paused. "As I said, my car broke down, and – and this man came to my assistance."

"I see."

"He offered me – shelter, for the night, and I accepted."

"Go on."

"Well, in the morning, the – the weather was worse, and I stayed on."

"Alone – with this man?"

"No. Not alone. He – he had a manservant. There were the three of us."

"And you stayed there all week?"

"Yes."

"And you fell in love with him?"

"Yes."

"So why did you come away?"

"He – he asked me to leave."

"My God!" Mike raised his eyes heavenward. "Why? What did you do?"

"I didn't do anything." Helen couldn't meet his eyes.

155

"Look, Mike, I've told you what happened –"

"A version of it, perhaps."

"What do you mean?"

"Oh, Helen! Why would this man ask you to stay on at his house if he didn't like you? And why would he suddenly ask you to leave? It doesn't make sense. Is he – was he very attractive?"

Helen sighed. "He – he had a limp. It troubled him a lot."

"He was a cripple?"

"Not exactly. He needed plenty of rest."

"And this is the man you've fallen in love with?" Mike was clearly astounded. "A man you say doesn't like you, and who's crippled into the bargain! Dear heaven, Helen, I wouldn't have thought – that is –"

Helen looked up then. "I know what you're trying to say, Mike," she said clearly. "You can't imagine why I should find such a man attractive when I could marry someone with perfect physical health and a healthy bank balance into the bargain!"

"Something like that."

"I know." Helen moved her shoulders in a dismissive gesture. "My father would feel exactly the same, if I told him."

"I expect he would." Mike sounded totally confused.

"And that's why I haven't told him."

Mike nodded slowly. "I'm beginning to understand." He considered what she had told him a few moments longer and then he said: "Tell me, Helen – this – relationship you had with the man: was it an emotional one?"

"I expect you would call it that."

"But he wasn't interested?"

"No."

"Are you sure about that?"

Helen drew a trembling breath. "He told me to leave, didn't he?"

"Yes." Mike drew a pattern on the tablecloth with his spoon. "But have you considered that his reasons for sending you away might have to do with his – disability?"

"What do you mean?" Now Helen stared at him.

"Just that – it's possible that he feels his incapacity to be too great to ask anyone to share it."

"Oh, no – *no!*"

Helen refused to react to this new and disturbing possibility. It simply wasn't credible. Mike still didn't know all the facts, so how could he make any satisfactory assessment? He didn't know, for instance, that Dominic had not *invited* her to stay at his house – he had *confined* her there. He didn't know that since the terrible accident which had killed his brother and injured him, Dominic had spurned the company of women. And last, but by no means least, he didn't know of Dominic's intention to make love to her that final evening before she left, an intention which had only been thwarted by her own impulsive confession of love for him. A love he had instantly rejected. Oh, no, Dominic was in no way crippled by his disability.

"So what *are* you going to do about it?"

Mike's voice brought her out of her reverie with a start. "Why – nothing, I suppose."

"You realise your father is still determined to find out where you were?"

"Did he tell you that?" Her eyes clouded. "Did he ask you to find out as much as you could?"

"Yes." Mike was honest.

Helen nodded. "I guessed as much."

"You know you can trust me, don't you?" His fingers were warm on hers.

"Oh, yes," she nodded, managing a faint smile. "Or I shouldn't be here."

CHAPTER NINE

ALTHOUGH Helen had rebuffed Mike's suggestion that Dominic might have had a motive for sending her away, during the next few days she found herself constantly going over the possibility in her mind. What if there was some truth in it? What if he was waiting for her to make the next move? He had said that she would forget all about him once she returned to London. Perhaps it was up to her to prove that she had not.

Schemes, all of them discarded, plagued her mind and it was only when Isabel made her opinion known that Helen finally came to a decision.

It was over breakfast one morning about a week later. Her father had already left for the office and Helen and Isabel were dawdling over their coffee. Isabel was still not dressed and in a transparent black negligée was looking particularly attractive as she cupped her chin on her hands and surveyed her stepdaughter across the table.

"You look ghastly," she announced brutally. "For God's sake, Helen, go and see this man, whoever he is!"

Helen's lips parted. "What man?"

"Oh, don't give me that!" Isabel reached for a cigarette. "This man who's giving you sleepless nights. You needn't bother to pretend that it's not a man. I've been there too many times myself not to recognise the symptoms!"

Helen looked down at her hands. "Has my father asked you to speak to me, Isabel?"

"Of course not. Do you honestly suppose your father would imagine *I* could influence you one way or the other?"

"Perhaps not."

"So. Why don't you go and see him? Whoever he is. He must be quite a man. I've never seen you like this before?"

Helen sighed. "You make it sound so easy."

"And isn't it? What's wrong? Is he married?"

"No!"

"So what's stopping you?"

Helen looked across at her stepmother square. "Nothing," she said evenly, coming to a decision. "Nothing at all."

Isabel half smiled. "Do I take it you'll be disappearing for another few days?"

"You can take it how you like."

"Well, don't worry about it. I'll tell Philip you've gone to stay with a girl friend for a few days. How does that sound?"

Helen rose to her feet. "Like a dream," she remarked, with some sarcasm.

Isabel chuckled. "Darling, I only want you to be happy."

"Do you?" Helen walked towards the door. "And off your back, too?"

"It's a tantalising possibility."

Helen shook her head and went out of the room. Isabel

could always be relied upon to speak her mind. All the same, if she could allay her father's suspicions, all the better.

It was nearing lunchtime before Helen could get away to begin her journey north to Hawksmere. She had brought an overnight bag because whatever happened she would be too tired to drive straight back to town that night. She felt pretty confident she could find her way to the house once she reached the village and got her whereabouts, and at least there was no snow now to hamper her progress. It was still visible of course, in the ditches and on the mountain slopes as she reached the lakeland area, but the roads were free of it, and here, as in London, trees and hedges were burgeoning with new life.

She reached Hawksmere in the late afternoon and as she drove through the village she kept her eyes alert for any small hotel which might take overnight guests. There was one, the Swan, and she made a note of it in case of emergencies. Her lips tightened. Would Dominic bar her the house after she had driven all this way? Would he refuse to see her? She hardly dared to speculate, and drove on quickly before discretion got the better of valour.

It was almost easy finding the rambling old house in daylight, but the daylight wouldn't last much longer and she put on a spurt of speed as she drove up to the heavy front door. There was no sign of life as she approached, no smoke coming from the chimneys, no sound of animals from the back.

She stopped the car and got out, quivering as she

looked up at the blank windows. Well, she was here, and the sooner she made her presence known the better.

She was tempted to turn the handle and open the door, but the thought that Sheba might be behind that door deterred her. Instead, she knocked and waited patiently for Bolt to answer.

But no one answered. The sound of her knocking echoed hollowly through the building and a wave of anticlimactic disappointment swept over her. She had been right in her earlier assumption. The place was deserted. They had gone!

She tried the door in the vain hope that she might be mistaken, but it was securely locked, and a swift reconnaissance of the yard at the back assured her that the animals had gone, too. But where? And when? And why? She sighed frustratedly. Had he imagined she would go telling her father where he was the minute she got back? Didn't he have any faith in her at all?

With depression like an actual physical presence bearing her down she got back into the car and drove back to the village. She passed only one car on her journey, a plain grey limousine, but its occupant was short and fair and plump, and bore no resemblance to either Dominic Lyall or Bolt.

The manager of the Swan Hotel was more than willing to accommodate her, and after being shown to a small, but attractive, bedroom under the eaves, Helen went down to take dinner in the small dining room. There appeared to be only one other guest, a short fair man with a moustache, and she was almost sure he was the man she had seen earlier on when she was leaving the house. But she

162

had too many things to ponder to pay much attention to that rather insignificant individual, and when the meal was over she deliberately engaged the manager in conversation.

"Tell me," she said encouragingly, "that – er – house, up the road a short way –"

"Ashbourn House, you mean, miss?"

"If that's its name. A rather rambling old building, but attractive, too."

"That's it, miss. You interested in it?"

"I – well, yes, I suppose I am."

The manager shook his head regretfully. "You'll have seen that it's empty. But it's not for sale."

"No?"

"No. The chap who owns it, he's away, that's all. I did hear he'd gone into hospital –"

"*Hospital*!" Helen spoke impulsively, and then forced herself to relax and smile at the man. "I mean – that's a pity. Was it something serious?"

The manager shrugged. "Can't rightly say, miss. We never did see much of them."

"Them?" probed Helen.

"Yes. This chap had a man living with him. Kind of batman, I suppose you'd call him. Name of Bolt. Used to come down to the village for supplies." He smiled. "Not that that's of any interest to you, miss."

"Oh – oh, but it is. Do go on."

The manager gave her a funny look. "You know this chap, maybe?" he suggested, and Helen was glad to bury her face in her coffee cup, shaking her head vigorously. "Well, anyway," went on her companion, "I expect they'll be coming back. Not much point in you hoping they'll be prepared to sell."

"No." Helen was wondering how she could phrase her next question. "It seems a pity the house is standing empty, though. I mean, I'd have thought this – what was it you said he was called? – Bolt? Well, I should have thought this man Bolt would have stayed at the house. To take care of things while his employer was in hospital, if they are coming back."

"Ah, yes. But as I hear it, they've gone to London. Perhaps this chap had to go into hospital there."

"*London!*"

Helen felt weak. To think she had driven all this way and Dominic was in some hospital in London! But why? What was wrong with him? She felt like climbing back into her car and driving straight back to town.

But of course she couldn't, and as the manager moved away to speak to the other occupant of the dining room, she rose and went up to her room. She would have an early night instead, and tomorrow she would leave first thing in the morning.

She slept better that night than she had done for weeks. She felt sure it was due to the exhausting journey, and the fact that she had drawn a blank. She felt utterly worn out.

But next morning, she felt refreshed, and drove back to town with more enthusiasm than she had left. Fortunately, both her father and Isabel were out when she reached home, and she was glad to let Bessie make her an omelette before beginning the task of finding out which hospital Dominic might be in. She was determined not to think too much about the reasons that might have put him

164

into hospital, but all the same as she rang hospital after hospital and drew a blank at all of them, the strain began to tell.

She was lying back wearily in her chair, her eyes aching from scanning telephone directories, when her father came in. She looked up tentatively, and saw that he was looking furious.

"What the hell do you think you're doing?" he demanded, kicking at one of the enormous directories she had left lying on the soft brown pile carpet.

Helen sighed. "Making telephone calls," she replied quietly.

"I can see that. Who are you ringing?"

"Does it matter? Can't I even make a telephone call now without asking you first?"

"Don't be impudent!" Her father thrust his hands into the pockets of his trousers. "Why did you drive to Hawksmere yesterday?"

Helen's mouth opened in surprise. "How do you know – oh, *no*! You didn't have me followed?"

"Why not? You've had a detective following you for the past three weeks," retorted her father laconically.

Helen's lips trembled. "I see."

Her father halted in front of her, looking down at her impatiently. "Are you going to tell me why you went to Hawksmere? Or shall I tell you?"

"You – *know*?"

"I think so." Her father breathed out heavily. "I think you went to see a man you thought was living at Ashbourn House. Dominic Lyall!"

Helen shaded her eyes with an unsteady hand. "Oh,

Daddy!" she exclaimed tremulously. "Why couldn't you just let well alone?"

"Helen, you're my daughter, my only offspring. Do you think I intend to sit back and allow you to ruin your life, the life I've got planned for you —"

"I'm twenty-two, Daddy —"

"What's that got to do with anything? You're still my daughter, and I have a right to know what you're doing."

"Daddy, you don't understand —"

"I understand perfectly. Now!" He flexed his shoulder muscles. "What did you hope to achieve by going to see Lyall? Is he the man you spent that week with?"

"Is there any point in denying it?"

"Not really. Barclay is very efficient."

"I suppose he was that nondescript little man in the restaurant last night."

"Yes, I suppose you might call him that. Private detectives usually are — nondescript, I mean. They need to be. The job calls for it. It wouldn't do for people to start noticing them."

"No, I suppose not."

"So you didn't find him, then?"

"No."

"Not surprising really, considering he's here in London."

Helen blinked as an idea occurred to her. "Do you know where in London?"

"I might do."

Helen sat bolt upright. "Oh, Daddy, please! Where is he?"

Her father frowned. "Why should I tell you?"

"Oh, Daddy!"

"All right. I'll tell you – he's in a private clinic."

"How did you find out?"

"Barclay is a little more efficient than you, my dear. He asked at the post office for the forwarding address."

"Oh, God!" Helen clenched her fists frustratedly. "Why didn't I think of that?"

"I doubt whether they'd have told you. But it's amazing how official a private detective's identity card can seem."

Helen shook her head. "I want to see him."

"I don't think that's a very good idea."

"*You* don't?" Helen got to her feet. "Daddy, I'll tell you this – if you don't tell me where he is, I'll walk out of this house now and you'll never see me again!"

"*Helen*!" Her father bit out the word. "Helen, for God's sake, stop behaving like a little fool! What does this man Lyall mean to you? What do you mean to him? How in God's name did you get to know him?"

"If I tell you, will you tell me where he is?"

Her father's nostrils drew in. "Very well. Providing you tell me the whole truth."

Helen hesitated, and then, sinking down on to the edge of her chair again, she slowly related the events which had led to her meeting with Dominic Lyall. She told of the blizzard, of her car's breaking down, and the appalling conditions that led to her going with him to his house. She explained how his face had seemed familiar and how inevitably she had recognised him.

At this point her father interrupted her, saying: "You don't mean this man is – *was* Dominic Lyall, the racing driver?" He sounded staggered.

Helen faltered. "Well – yes. I thought you knew."

"Helen, Helen! It's not such an unusual name. I never dreamed . . ." He shook his head. "I'm sorry. Go on."

Helen went on, more enthusiastically now, sensing that her father's antagonism had somehow eased. Of course, he had been such a fan of Dominic Lyall. Was it possible that he still admired him?

Leaving out the intimate details of her relationship with Dominic, and yet hinting at what had happened, she finished her story, and only then did her father expel his breath in a long whistle.

"God!" he muttered. "What a situation!"

"Now do you understand why I couldn't tell you?"

"You could have trusted me."

"Could I?" Helen looked sceptical and Philip had the grace to look shamefaced.

"Well, maybe you have some reason to think otherwise," he admitted, shaking his head. "But, Helen, Dominic Lyall must be nearly forty!"

"I think he's thirty-eight," she conceded, nodding. "What does that matter?"

Her father shook his head again. "He's too old for you. And besides, you say he's crippled!"

"Oh, Daddy, don't use that word!" She licked her lips. "He has a limp. Do you think I care? If he had to spend his days in a wheelchair, I'd still love him!"

Philip left her to go and pour himself a drink, but when he raised his glass in a silent question, she shook her head.

"Not for me, thanks." She stood up again. "Now will you tell me where he is?"

"In a minute, in a minute." Her father swallowed half

168

the whisky he had poured in a single gulp. "Do you know why he's in hospital?"

"No. Do you?"

"No. We haven't got that far in our investigations. For the moment I've told Barclay to call a halt."

"Thank God for that!"

"What do you mean?"

"Oh, Daddy, how do you think he's going to feel when he finds out you've been spying on him? He – he'll think I've told you."

"You have!"

"You know what I mean." Helen moved impatiently. "Daddy, are you going to tell me where he is?"

"Oh, very well." Her father pulled a card out of his inside pocket. "This is the clinic. It's run by a Doctor Jorge Johannsen. I know little about it except that he's reputed to be an expert orthopaedic surgeon."

"An orthopaedic surgeon!" Helen paled. "Oh, Daddy, do you think he's entered this clinic for an operation on his hip?"

"How should I know?" Her father shifted impatiently. "If you're determined to see him, I suggest you go round there and find out for yourself."

Helen nodded dazedly. "Yes. Yes, I'll do that." She hurried to the door. "Thank you, Daddy."

Philip hunched his shoulders irritably. "Don't thank me. I'm making no promises. But if seeing this man can put a bit of life back into you, I'm prepared to go along with that."

Helen hesitated a moment, wanting to say more, but then with a shake of her head she left him.

The Johannsen Clinic stood in Harley Street. It had once been a luxurious town house, but now its three upper floors and basement had been converted into an expensively equipped private hospital. Helen dismissed her taxi and climbed the steps to the door. Inside, a small lobby gave on to a reception area, and she pressed the button that indicated *Attention* on the desk.

She stood looking about her curiously, trying not to think of the reasons why she was there. Flowers gave the formality of the reception desk a touch of elegance, and their perfume dissipated any clinical odour. The hall which gave on to the staircase was carpeted in soft olive green, and the plain cream walls were hung with prints. It was really more like the reception hall of a hotel, and Helen tried to pretend its associations were just as innocent.

"Helen!"

The shocked ejaculation interrupted her thoughts and she swung round to find Bolt descending the last few stairs between them.

"Oh, Bolt!" she exclaimed, and her voice had a distinct tremor. "Bolt – is Dominic here?"

In a plain grey suit Bolt looked strangely formal and unfamiliar, but when he saw the anxiety in her face, his own features relaxed. "Yes," he replied quietly. "He's here."

Helen went towards him, looking up at him imploringly. "How is he? Why is he here? Bolt, did – did carrying me do this?"

Bolt glanced round. "Has anyone attended to you?"

"No. There was no one about. I rang the bell, but no

170

one has come."

He glanced at his watch. "It's teatime. The patients are served tea at five o'clock. I expect everyone's busy." He nodded towards a room marked "Visitors". "We'll go in here. There's not likely to be anyone waiting about at this time of day."

It was true. The comfortable lounge was empty. Bolt closed the door and then when Helen refused to do as he suggested and sit down, he said: "What are you doing here?"

Helen sighed. "I want to see Dominic."

"How did you know he was here?"

"It's a long story. Bolt, please, won't you get to the point? Why is Dominic here?"

Bolt thrust his hands into his trousers' pockets. "He decided to have the operation they wanted him to have after the accident," he stated heavily.

"You mean – you mean he agreed to have an artificial piece of bone grafted into his hip!" Helen was staggered.

"Something like that."

"Oh, Bolt!" Helen pressed her palms to her cheeks. "And when – when does he have the operation?"

"He had it two weeks ago."

"Two weeks?" Helen couldn't take it in. "But that was – that was –"

"– just after you left, yes."

Helen stared at him confusedly. "Why did he suddenly decide to have the operation?"

Bolt looked down at the polished toes of his shoes. "I really don't know."

Helen caught his arm. "I don't believe you," she exclaimed tremulously. "Dominic would be bound to discuss it with you!"

"And is it any concern of yours?" asked Bolt quietly.

Helen's eyes were unusually bright. "I think so. I – I love him."

Bolt shook his head. "Do you?"

"Yes. Yes!" Helen spread her hands. "All right, all right, if you won't tell me why he did it, at least tell me if it's a success."

Bolt hesitated. "If I do, you must promise not to tell him what I've said."

"Of course." A little worried frown had appeared on Helen's wide brow. From the tone of his voice, she already knew the answer.

"Then – no," he admitted reluctantly. "They couldn't do it."

Helen's shoulders sagged. "Do you know why?"

"I don't know all the medical jargon, but basically it seems that if a bone is allowed to heal without repair it becomes a potential source of deformity to other joints. In this case the lapse of time between the injury and its treatment had led to a more difficult condition."

"Oh, Bolt!" Helen felt an overwhelming sense of compassion for the man she loved. "Oh, where is he? I must see him!"

Bolt sighed. "I don't know whether he'll agree to see you, Helen."

"Why not?"

"I think you know why not."

Helen walked to the door. "I'm going to see him," she said clearly, even though her voice still shook. "And no one's going to stop me."

When she emerged into the hall again with Bolt behind her, the receptionist was at her desk. She looked at Helen in surprise and Bolt went ahead of her, saying: "This is a – friend of Mr. Lyall's. Is it possible for her to see him now?"

Helen felt an immense amount of gratitude towards Bolt for his intervention. His introduction made her presence there so much less difficult to explain, and the receptionist smiled and nodded and said she was sure it would be all right. She sent for a nurse to escort the visitor to Dominic's room and Bolt gave Helen a reassuring pat on the shoulder before she and the nurse entered the cage-like lift which transported them to the second floor. Here the corridor was rubber-tiled, silent and efficient, and there was a distinctly clinical atmosphere which had not been evident downstairs. Dominic's room was at the end of this corridor, and the young nurse opened his door and said brightly: "You've got a visitor, Mr. Lyall. Come in, Miss James."

Helen entered with some misgivings, half prepared for Dominic to order her away. But although he did not smile, he said nothing to embarrass her until the nurse had left them alone. He was sitting up in the narrow bed wearing dark red silk pyjamas, and Helen could not drag her eyes away from him. It seemed so much longer than three weeks since she had seen him and she was hungry for the sight of him. She scarcely noticed the pleasant room with its pale blue carpet, and deeper blue bedspread and curtains, so much more attractive than any ordinary hospital room, and when the nurse closed the door she started violently at the harshness in his voice.

"How the hell did you find me here?" he demanded.

She drew an unsteady breath. "Hello, Dominic," she murmured. "How – how are you?"

His lean face mirrored his irritation and her heart sank. "Did Bolt send for you?"

"No. No, of course not." She approached the bed, longing to touch the brown hand lying against the coverlet. The neck of his pyjama jacket was open and she could see the hair at the base of his throat. It was a devastating thought that he had held her in his arms, close against the hard strength of his body, and she longed for him to hold her again. "Dominic, I went to Hawksmere, and – and I found out that you'd come to London."

"Why did you go to Hawksmere?"

For a moment curiosity got the better of anger, and she answered eagerly: "I wanted to see you again –"

His lips twisted. "Really? Why?"

"Dominic, you know why –" Her voice broke and she reached for his fingers urgently, but he drew his hand away.

"I think you've made a mistake," he stated coldly. "I thought I made the position clear enough several weeks ago. You and I have nothing more to say to one another."

Helen caught her breath. "I don't believe that –"

"It makes no difference to me what you believe." A frown drew his brows together. "How did you find this hospital? I told no one." His lips curled. "Except Bolt!"

"It – wasn't – Bolt." Helen spoke with difficulty. "If – if you must know, my father had me followed. He – he's had me followed ever since I got back."

"What do you mean – followed?"

"What do you think I mean?" Her voice cracked on a sob. "He had a private detective trailing me. I told you what he was like. He – he tried to force me to tell him where I'd been when I got back."

"Why didn't you simply tell him you'd been staying at a hotel?"

"I did. But – but the hotel I mentioned, he'd had checked out. After that –" She made a helpless gesture.

Dominic's hands clenched into fists. "And I suppose it was this detective who found the clinic."

"Yes." Helen sighed. "But – but Daddy didn't really know who you are. Not until – not until I told him."

"You *told* him?" Dominic's eyes were narrowed to tawny slits.

"Yes. I *had* to." She shook her head. "He wouldn't tell me where you were until – until –"

Dominic glared unseeingly towards the windows. "Are you sure you're telling me the whole truth?" he muttered.

"What do you mean?"

"Well, are you sure it wasn't this detective who made the trip to Hawksmere? Who found out I was in hospital? Who put two and two together?"

Helen was confused. "I don't understand –"

His eyes turned back to her. "I think you do. Didn't you discover that I was in hospital for the operation to repair my hip?"

"I – well – yes –"

"I thought as much. And did you think I'd done it for you?"

"No, I – how could I?"

But she had. Vaguely such an idea had occurred to her after what Bolt had told her, and it was evident in her face.

"Who have you spoken to since you came here?" he demanded.

"Why, no – no one."

"Good. I don't want you discussing my condition with anyone, do you understand? My affairs are no concern of yours. I'm sorry to disappoint you, but when I get out of here I have no intention of using my new-found freedom to seek you out."

"Your – new-found – freedom?"

"Of course. You don't know, do you? The operation was a complete success. I should be as good as new in a couple of months. What a pity you won't be around to share in the celebrations, but I'll send you a card from Florida or Jamaica or wherever else the fancy takes me!"

Helen was frozen to the spot. What was he saying? That the operation had succeeded in righting his hip? That he would not be limping when he left the hospital? But Bolt had said that it had failed, that the deformity was such that it could not be cured!

She felt sick. One of them was lying – but which? And did it matter anyway? Dominic didn't want her, he had made that perfectly clear, so why delay the inevitable? She had to get out of there – the sooner the better.

She half turned towards the door. It seemed a long distance away, but she could make it. She had to. She would not break down in front of him. That would be the final straw.

She moved unsteadily across the pale blue carpet, and when her hand reached the handle he said: "Don't worry about your father learning of my existence. I'm sure when you tell him what has happened he'll be only too willing to keep the information to himself."

Helen cast one last look over her shoulder. There were lines of strain beside his mouth and now as she looked at him with despairing eyes she saw how much thinner he had become. Oh, God, she thought desperately, why did she care so much? Let him go on and live his life the way he chose. She would not think about him any more.

CHAPTER TEN

To her relief Bolt was not around when she left the building. Almost in a daze, she summoned a taxi and gave the address of her father's house, but halfway there she changed the destination to the Embankment. She knew the taxi driver looked at her strangely as she paid him off near Westminster Bridge, and she thought rather hysterically that he had the suspicion that she was about to do away with herself.

And the temptation was there as she looked down into the murky waters. She had never felt so low, and the knowledge that her father would be waiting for her at home, waiting for an explanation, filled her with depression. She didn't want to talk about the scene she had just had with Dominic, but she didn't see how she could avoid it.

The rush hour traffic of early evening passed her by as she wandered along, eventually going into a café and ordering herself some tea. It was almost seven o'clock before she made her way home and when the taxi stopped at the door her father came leaping down the steps to help her out.

"Oh, thank God!" he muttered, taking her arm and drawing her up the steps to the house. "Are you trying to give me a heart attack?"

Helen's mouth twitched at this. Her father seemed invincible somehow. "I'm sorry if you've been worried about me," she began, but he interrupted her.

"Worried about you?" he snapped. "Helen, do you realise you left the clinic over an hour and a half ago!"

"You rang, I suppose," she said wearily.

"Rang? Of course I rang. Where have you been?"

"I went for a walk – along the Embankment."

"The Embankment?" Her father paled slightly. "My God, Helen, you weren't – you weren't thinking of –"

"I did think of it, yes," she admitted quietly. "Oh, Daddy, I'm so miserable!"

And she burst into tears.

Some three hours later there was a ring at the bell of the James' house in Barbary Square. Helen was in bed, but not sleeping, even though the tablets her father had given her before leaving to take Isabel to a formal dinner at the Guildhall should have helped her to do so.

Since her return home that evening she had had to revise her opinion of her father somewhat. He had been so kind, so gentle, so understanding – and she realised that when it came right down to it he was just as concerned for her happiness as any other father might be.

Now she sat up in bed as the bell rang again and looked at her watch. It was almost ten-thirty. Who could be calling at this hour? Unless her father and stepmother had had an accident . . .

She slid out of bed, pulling on a pale green chiffon robe over her matching nightdresss. It was nearest thing to hand and she dared not delay any longer. Bessie was not in, she was alone in the house, and the idea that it might be a thief or an intruder of some sort hardly occurred to her.

She ran lightly down the stairs, crossed the hall and opened the door to the width of the safety chain. Then she gasped. Dominic was on the threshold – leaning heavily on a stick.

"Hello, Helen," he said, and the lines of strain she had seen earlier were etched more deeply beside his mouth. "May I come in? I'd like to talk to you."

Helen licked her lips and pressing the door closed for a moment released the chain. Then she stood back, concealing herself behind the door as he limped in. It was only then that she became aware of the scarcity of her attire and with a swiftly-drawn breath, she exclaimed: "I'll just go and put on some clothes –"

"No!" His hand reached out and caught her wrist as she would have passed him. His eyes surveyed her with disturbing appraisal. "No, don't go. I like you the way you are."

Helen's cheeks flamed. "Dominic –"

"Is there somewhere where we can talk?" He winced as a spasm of pain seemed to catch him unawares. "Could I – sit down?"

"Of course, of course. Do you want to lean on me?"

Her eyes were wide and concerned, but he shook his head, his expression a trifle wry. "I don't think that's necessary," he replied, but she saw that he leaned more heavily on the stick as she led the way into the lounge.

She switched on the lamps, and then hovered uncertainly by the door as he limped to the wide velvet-covered

180

couch and lowered himself with evident relief into its soft cushions. Then he turned to look at her and embarrassment took over again.

"I – must go and put something else on," she insisted, and he shrugged his broad shoulders.

"All right. If it pleases you to be modest. But I do have a pretty good idea of what a woman's body looks like."

Helen stared at him, her appearance forgotten. "Why – why have you come here?" she asked unevenly.

He lay back against the cushions, his lean face bearing a faint mockery now that the strain of walking had been taken from him. She thought, half despairingly, that she would never grow tired of looking at him – at his dark features, the silvery swathe of hair that persisted in falling across his forehead, the sensual curve of his mouth . . .

"Come here and I'll tell you," he said, and there was no mockery there now.

Helen took a couple of tentative steps and then halted. What was she doing? What was he doing? Why had he come here? Was this another way he had conceived of hurting her?

"Dominic –" she began again, and he leant forward impatiently and caught her wrist, jerking her down on top of him. She felt the hardness of his thighs beneath hers, the roughness of his hands against her flesh, and then his mouth was on hers and he was bearing her down against the soft velvet cushions with an urgency that brooked no denial. The weight of his body on hers was not a pain, it was a sensual pleasure, and her lips parted involuntarily while her whole body yielded to the throbbing pressure of his.

It was a long time before he let her go and when he did his eyes were still glazed with the intensity of his emotions. He forced himself up and looked down at her with slightly impatient eyes as he said: "Not here, Helen. Not like this. Do you want me to be making love to you when your father gets home?"

Helen stirred lethargically. "I don't mind," she murmured, stretching up a hand to touch his cheek. "Oh, Dominic, I love you . . ."

Dominic caught her hand and pressed his lips to the palm. "Helen, are you sure you know what you're saying?"

She nodded, but then something he had said caused her to blink rapidly and prop herself up on her elbows. "Dominic, did – did my father ask you to come here?"

Dominic released her hand and swinging his legs to the ground, sat up straight. "No. On the contrary, I don't think he sees the idea of me as a son-in-law as something to encourage."

Helen scrambled up on to her knees. "What – what did you just say?"

"I'm quite sure you heard me," he remarked, a faintly mocking expression appearing. "Oh, Helen, I love you! Surely you've realised that by now!"

"You – love – me?" Helen's lips trembled, her whole body quivered with an emotion stronger than herself. "Oh, Dominic, Dominic, why didn't you tell me?"

And she flung herself into his arms, burying her face in his neck, clinging to him blindly, tears of happiness and relief mingling on her cheeks.

"Hey – *hey!* " He held her loosely in his arms, stroking a lazy finger down her nose, licking the salty drops from her eyelids. "Helen, we have some talking to do, and if you go on like this I won't be able to say all that has to be said."

She sniffed. "All right." She sat back on her heels. "Go ahead. You've seen Daddy, haven't you?"

"Oh, yes, I saw your father earlier this evening. He was most concerned about the bad effect I was having on you. Look, I can understand how he feels. He hoped you'd find somebody much more suitable for a husband –"

"Stop it!" She put her fingers over his mouth. "I don't care what my father hopes. It's you I love. And – and –" She bent her head. "Bolt told me about – about the operation."

"Yes, I know that, too – *now,*" he murmured dryly.

She looked up. "How?"

"How do you think? Bolt confessed."

"You weren't – angry with him?"

"What do you think?" Dominic suddenly pulled her close to him again. "Oh, God, Helen, I tried to deny myself – I really tried. I kept telling myself that I couldn't think of tying you to a cripple for the rest of your life, but then – then this evening . . ." He shook his head, burying his face in her neck and she felt him shudder. "When Bolt told me that you'd known – before you came to see me –" He cupped her face in his hands. "I thought – I really thought you'd only come because you thought I was going to be – normal –"

Helen slid her arms round his neck. "You are normal!

183

Oh, Dominic, my love for you doesn't hinge on whether you walk with a limp or without one! I don't care. I love you." Her lips quivered. "Although why I should after the way you treated me –"

His mouth caressed hers. "Was I so bad – all the time?"

"No," she conceded with a slight deepening of entrancing colour. "Not all the time."

"I almost lost control that morning in the sauna," he admitted huskily. "I shouldn't have let you do what you did."

"Didn't you enjoy it?"

"Too much." He smiled at her embarrassment. "Promise me you'll do it again when we're married."

"Every day if you like," she agreed eagerly, but he shook his head.

"No. I think for the moment Bolt will have to keep his job. If you don't mind?"

"Of course not." She took a deep breath. It was all so wonderful she could hardly take it in. "Can we live where – where *you* live?"

"That's a long way from London."

"So?" She frowned.

"Well –" He paused. "Won't you want to be nearer civilisation? I mean –"

"Do you want to live here, in London?"

"Helen, I'd made up my mind that if that's what you want –"

"But what about you? You don't really want to live here, do you?"

He touched her cheek. "I don't want to cut you off from your friends – your family –"

184

"I'd like to live at Ashbourn House," she stated simply. "I can think of nothing more desirable than living there – really living there – with you."

Dominic's eyes darkened and for a few minutes there was silence in the lamplit room. But then he determinedly put her away from him, saying thickly: "Perhaps you should put some clothes on, Helen. I intend to stay until I've spoken to your father, and I shouldn't like to shock him. Who knows, maybe he won't be too disappointed after all . . ."

Six months later Helen came down the stairs of the house near Hawksmere amid the glory of a sunlit September evening. She was looking particularly lovely, she knew that, and the long amber-coloured maternity dress successfully concealed her condition from all but the most discerning eye. She glanced up the stairs, but there was no sign as yet of her father or Isabel and with a smile at her reflection in the hall mirror she entered the living room.

Dominic was standing by the bureau, mixing drinks as she entered, lean and attractive in a dark dinner jacket. He had recovered completely from the operation now and no longer needed the stick he had had to use in the beginning. His eyes flickered over her with a disturbing penetration and he left what he was doing to go to her, pulling her possessively into his arms.

"You're looking particularly beautiful this evening," he murmured against her mouth. "Are you going to tell them?"

Helen drew back and smiled. "That they're going to be

185

grandparents in five months? Do you think I should?"

Dominic's mouth curved a little amusedly. "You may not have to. I'm sure Isabel has already guessed. Didn't you notice the way she was looking at you earlier? Just after they arrived? Smocks and slacks may look casual, but you're beginning to have that certain look – that certain *je ne sais quoi*."

Helen stroked his cheek. "Do you mind?"

His arms tightened and he buried his face in her neck. "Well, I could say that I would have preferred to have you to myself for a little while longer," he said in a muffled voice. "But as I'm responsible..." His hands curved possessively over her hips. "You go to my head! Precautions never entered into it."

Helen slid her arms round his neck, no longer embarrassed by what he said. "I expect Bolt will make a marvellous nursemaid."

"Could be." Dominic lifted his head with reluctance. "Oh, damn, I think someone's coming. Why did we ever come home? I don't like sharing you with anyone."

Helen sighed contentedly. "Darling, we were away almost four months. Daddy naturally wants to assure himself that I'm happy."

"Hmm." Dominic moved back to the cocktail shaker. "And what will you tell him? That I beat you? That I make your life a misery?"

"Do you think if I did he'd believe me?" she exclaimed, stretching her arms above her head.

Dominic's eyes rested on her stomach. "Perhaps not," he agreed, gently mocking. "It's just as well Sheba's not here any more. She might have aroused some suspicions."

186

Helen laughed, and then there was a knock at the door and she turned, calling: "Come in, Bolt."

The burly manservant entered the room diffidently, but the warm enveloping smile he reserved for Helen was eloquent of his approval of their relationship.

"What time shall I serve dinner, sir?" he enquired politely.

Dominic glanced at his watch. "In about half an hour, I think, thank you, Bolt. Oh, and by the way, how are you at washing nappies?"

Bolt's dark brows, the only hairy thing about his head, lifted in astonishment. "I – I – you don't mean –"

"He does." Helen went towards him smilingly. "And we wanted you to be among the first to know."

Bolt's expression was frankly delighted. "I couldn't be more pleased," he exclaimed, going to shake Dominic's hand. "Congratulations!"

Dominic handed him a glass. "Here," he said. "Have a drink. It's not every day I become an expectant father."

Bolt took the glass and raised it warmly. "To the new generation of Lyalls," he said, and Dominic said he would drink to that.

BARBARA DELINSKY
Fingerprints

Carly Quinn is a
woman with a past.
Born Robyn Hart, she
was forced to don a new
identity when her intensive
investigation of an arson-ring
resulted in a photographer's death
and threats against her life.

Ryan Cornell's entrance into her life
was a gradual one. The handsome
lawyer's interest was piqued, and then
captivated, by the mysterious Carly — a
woman of soaring passions and a
secret past.

RIDE A PAINTED PONY

by **BEVERLY SOMMERS**
The third
HARLEQUIN AMERICAN ROMANCE
PREMIER EDITION

A prestigious New York City publishing
company decides to launch a new historical
romance line, led by a woman who must first
define what love means.

At your favorite retail store or send your name,
address and zip or postal code, along with a check or
money order for $3.70 (includes 75¢ for postage and
handling) payable to Harlequin Reader Service to:

Harlequin Reader Service

In the U.S.
Box 52040
Phoenix, AZ
85072-2040

In Canada
5170 Yonge Street
P.O. Box 2800, Postal Station A,
Willowdale, Ontario   M2N 5T5

Harlequin reaches into the hearts and minds of women across America to bring you

Harlequin American Romance ™·

YOURS FREE!

Enter a uniquely exciting new world with

Harlequin American Romance T.M.

Harlequin American Romances are the first romances to explore today's love relationships. These compelling novels reach into the hearts and minds of women across America... probing the most intimate moments of romance, love and desire.

You'll follow romantic heroines and irresistible men as they boldly face confusing choices: Career first, love later? Love without marriage? Long-distance relationships? All the experiences that make love real are captured in the tender, loving pages of **Harlequin American Romances.**

What makes American women so different when it comes to love? Find out with **Harlequin American Romance!**

Send for your introductory FREE book now!

Get this book FREE!

Mail to:

Harlequin Reader Service

In the U.S.
2504 West Southern Ave.
Tempe, AZ 85282

In Canada
P.O. Box 2800, Postal Station A
5170 Yonge St., Willowdale, Ont. M2N 5T5

YES! I want to be one of the first to discover **Harlequin American Romance.** Send me FREE and without obligation *Twice in a Lifetime.* If you do not hear from me after I have examined my FREE book, please send me the 4 new **Harlequin American Romances** each month as soon as they come off the presses. I understand that I will be billed only $2.25 for each book (total $9.00). There are no shipping or handling charges. There is no minimum number of books that I have to purchase. In fact, I may cancel this arrangement at any time. *Twice in a Lifetime* is mine to keep as a FREE gift, even if I do not buy any additional books.   154 BPA NAXG

_____

Name   (please print)

_____

Address   Apt. no.

_____

City   State/Prov.   Zip/Postal Code

_____

Signature (If under 18, parent or guardian must sign.)

This offer is limited to one order per household and not valid to current Harlequin American Romance subscribers. We reserve the right to exercise discretion in granting membership. If price changes are necessary, you will be notified.
Offer expires May 31, 1985